MEDICINE WOMAN

The grizzly bear had done quite a job on Golden Hawk. His skin had been laid open to the bone. It felt like a rib had been cracked inside him. And fever was consuming him like raging fire gone out of control.

He tried to tell the Indian girl, Singing Wind, that he was a goner. But she wouldn't listen.

He felt her hand stroking him and he groaned and tried to turn his head away. But she pushed his head toward her and closed her lips about his. Her arms enclosed him fiercely and she pressed against him, rocking his naked body back and forth.

Dimly he felt a spark of arousal from some-where deep within him.

This treatment was going to kill or cure him— but even if it failed, it was going to be a helluva way to die. . . .

ROUGH RIDERS

☐ **THEY CAME TO CORDURA by Glendon Swarthout.** The classic Western by the author of *The Shootist*. Major Thorn was supposed to be a coward, the five men under him were supposed to be heroes, and the woman they guarded was supposed to be a wench. But as the outlaw army closed in on them in the heat of the desert, the odds could change— and so could the people. "Excitement from start to finish."—*The New York Times* (146581—$2.75)

☐ **SKINNER by F.M. Parker.** John Skinner never really liked to kill—until now ... against a thieving, murdering gang that held the woman he loved for ransom. Wild and tough as the mustangs he bred in the harshest badlands in the West, Skinner yearned to have the ruthless gang in his sights. Pulling the trigger was going to be a pleasure.... (138139—$2.75)

☐ **OUTLAW'S EMPIRE by Ray Hogan.** With every man's gun against him, Riley Tabor had to think quick and draw fast. Riley was a cattle driver not a gunslinger—until he had to shoot down a vicious hardcase to save the life of an Eastern greenhorn. Wanted by the law, he headed into territory where no one knew what he had done ... and got hired to rid the land of an outlaw army. But his past caught up with him and put him in the middle of a crossfire.... (148274—$2.75)

☐ **THE RAWHIDERS by Ray Hogan.** Forced outside the law, Matt Buckman had to shoot his way back in. Rescued from the savage Kiowas by four men who appeared suddenly to save him, Matt Buckman felt responsible for the death of one and vowed to ride in his place. Soon he discovered that filling the dead man's boots would not be easy ... he was riding with a crew of killers ... killers he owed his life to....(143922—$2.75)

GOLDEN HAWK 3

GRIZZLY PASS

Will C. Knott

A SIGNET BOOK

NEW AMERICAN LIBRARY

PUBLISHER'S NOTE

This novel is a work of fiction. Names, characters, places, and incidents either are the product of the author's imagination or are used fictitiously, and any resemblance to actual persons, living or dead, events, or locales is entirely coincidental.

NAL BOOKS ARE AVAILABLE AT QUANTITY DISCOUNTS WHEN USED TO PROMOTE PRODUCTS OR SERVICES. FOR INFORMATION PLEASE WRITE TO PREMIUM MARKETING DIVISION, NEW AMERICAN LIBRARY, 1633 BROADWAY, NEW YORK, NEW YORK 10019.

SIGNET TRADEMARK REG. U.S. PAT. OFF. AND FOREIGN COUNTRIES
REGISTERED TRADEMARK—MARCA REGISTRADA
HECHO EN CHICAGO, U.S.A.

SIGNET, SIGNET CLASSIC, MENTOR, ONYX, PLUME, MERIDIAN and NAL BOOKS are published by New American Library, 1633 Broadway, New York, New York 10019

First Signet Printing, March, 1987

1 2 3 4 5 6 7 8 9

PRINTED IN THE UNITED STATES OF AMERICA

GOLDEN HAWK

A quiet stream under the Comanche moon . . . leaping savages . . . knives flashing in the firelight . . . brutal, shameful death . . .

Ripped from the bosom of their slain parents and carried off by the raiding Comanches, Jed Thompson and his sister can never forget that hellish night under the glare of the Comanche moon, seared into their memories forever. Years later, Golden Hawk now, his vengeance slaked, Jed is pursued relentlessly by his past Comanche brothers and driven by only one purpose: to recapture his sister from those who would bend her proud beauty to their savage will.

Golden Hawk. Half Comanche, half white man. A legend in his time, an awesome nemesis to some—a bulwark and a refuge to any man or woman lost in the terror of that raw, savage land.

— 1 —

It all happened so fast Hawk was unable to save the Indian.

He had been moving down a steep slope, his eye on the Crow and on the elk the Indian's flintlock had brought down, when a monstrous male grizzly charged out of the brush, heading on a beeline for the downed elk and the Indian. It was close to winter, the grizzly's most ravenous feeding time as he readied himself for his long sleep, and the scent of the freshly killed elk had evidently drawn him on the run. Before the hapless Indian could get out of the way, the bear sprang upon him and began to maul him fearfully, the bear's great talons ripping the Crow from shoulder to crotch while his canines closed about the Crow's head and face, tearing at them with a terrible fury. The blood spurted from the Crow's wounds, darkening the bear's silvery pelt.

Hawk plunged down the rest of the slope and dashed across the small clearing to where the Crow and the grizzly were locked in their terrible embrace. His rifle was already charged. Slamming the Hawken's muzzle against the bear's head just behind the ear, Hawk pulled the trigger. The rifle detonated, but a second before it did, the bear turned his head, knocking aside the barrel.

The round struck the bear's snout, ripping through it. With a howl of pain and outrage, the grizzly released the Crow and went for Hawk. Backing up hastily, Hawk pulled out his Walker and emptied his last four rounds at the great humped beast. All four rounds slammed into the bear's chest. They slowed the beast momentarily, but they did not stop him. He swiped the empty Walker from Hawk's hand, the bear's eight-inch talon opening a flap of skin clear to Hawk's elbow.

Ignoring the wound, Hawk unsheathed his bowie and stood his ground as the bear charged. One vicious swipe of the bear's right paw opened Hawk's left side. And then the great beast was upon Hawk, crushing against him with terrible force. Hawk felt a rib crack under the enormous pressure as he began to plunge his knife into the enraged beast's back and neck. Over and over his blade slipped deep into the bear's hide while the awful, crushing pressure of the bear's grip in-

creased. Hawk felt another rib snap as he continued to slash at the bear with no visible effect.
Suddenly, as if annoyed with Hawk and the game
he was playing, the grizzly stepped back, caught
Hawk with his left paw, and flung him aside like
a piece of carrion.

Hawk landed heavily on his back, managing
somehow to hang on to the bowie. Dazed, bleeding from his wounds, he stared up at the slavering, bleeding jaws of the huge carnivore, no longer
confident that he or his bowie could do anything
more than irritate this monster. But the bear had
been wounded, perhaps mortally. His chest was
a tangled black mat of fur from the gunshot
wounds.

The problem was that the animal didn't really
know how badly he was hurt. Rearing unsteadily
up onto his hind legs, he uttered a fearsome roar,
then came down hard onto his four feet and
shambled woozily toward Hawk, peering meanly
at him out of small, squinting black eyes, evidently determined to finish him off. Scrambling
to his feet, Hawk looked about for a tree. But
there was none close enough.

He looked back at the bear and saw—beyond
the grizzly—the Crow stirring to life despite his
fearsome wounds. On the ground behind the bear,
the Indian snatched up his bow and fitted an
arrow to the bowstring. Seeing this, Hawk moved
quickly backward, keeping himself between the
bear and the Indian. The bear followed, shuf-

fling doggedly toward him, his shattered snout dripping.

Suddenly the bear roared in pain and swung about. The Crow's arrow had plunged deep into the grizzly's rectum. Taking advantage of the bear's momentary confusion, Hawk ran forward and leapt onto his back. Leaning over the bear's great hump, he plunged the long blade of his bowie repeatedly into the side of the bear's neck. Yet even when the blood gouted from the bear's neck, proving Hawk had severed his jugular, this appeared to have no effect on the huge animal.

Swinging about wildly, the bear dislodged Hawk and flung him to the ground. On his feet in an instant, Hawk raced desperately for the slope, hoping he could make the timber halfway up. A grizzly could not climb a tree, but by this time Hawk was wondering if he could either. With a great bark of anger, the grizzly took after him. Despite his own wounds and the searing pain in his chest from the two cracked ribs, Hawk neared the slope. The ground began to shake behind him as the great bear gained on Hawk. Then came the sound of something very heavy striking the ground.

Hawk glanced back.

The grizzly was down, his full length stretched out on the grass, his massive body covering an astonishing patch of the meadow. His head lifted for an instant and his small, beady eyes focused on Hawk. Then he let his head fall forward.

There was a single great, weary shudder, and the grizzly lay dead at Hawk's feet.

Slowly Hawk sank to the ground. As soon as he caught his breath, he examined his wounds. He was astonished at the clean precision of the long slashes that covered his body. On his right arm the neat rip ran from the base of his thumb clear to his elbow. Blood oozed steadily from it, gradually encasing the arm in a dark carapace. His left side had been opened up as well, and his left thigh was also encased as the blood mixed with his buckskin pants leg to form an even harder shell. Each intake of breath was a problem, sometimes causing him to cough, which in turn led him to spit up blood. The broken ribs must have punctured a lung, and the exertion of his run for the slope had seriously aggravated his condition.

Still, he was alive. His condition was perhaps not much better than that. But it was enough, and he would take it.

Hawk got carefully to his feet, not an easy task, as he was trying hard not to inhale or exhale too deeply. He would have to bind his ribs before long, he realized, or he might end up with a collapsed lung. He had seen Comanche warriors home from raids suffer terribly and sometimes die when that occurred. Once on his feet, Hawk moved carefully around the fallen bear and over to the Bannock Indian.

The Indian was still alive, stretched out on the ground, the bow still clutched in his hand. He lifted his head to look up at Hawk, and Hawk gasped. The grizzly had torn off the Indian's scalp from crown to eyebrows so that a great raw flap of it hung down over his face. Long, gaping slashes down the length of his body had laid the Crow open like a fish readied for the coals. A portion of his spine showed through at one spot and farther down Hawk caught a glimpse of the man's gray intestines flecked with blood working out from under his body, in time with his labored breathing.

The Crow must have been in considerable pain, but he uttered not a word of complaint.

Hawk spoke to him in Comanche, but the man could not speak Comanche and so replied in his own tongue. Hawk shook his head. He could not follow this particular Crow dialect, though he was now becoming almost fluent in Crow as well as some Blackfoot and Nez Perće dialects, too. Since his wound made it impossible to use sign language, the Crow spoke in a crude English, the effort to speak obviously sapping his strength.

"Me . . . Crow Feather."

"I'm Jed Thompson."

"No. You Golden Hawk."

Hawk was, as always, surprised and even disturbed at his widespread fame—or infamy. There was not a tribe in the Plains or in these high Rockies that did not know of him, it seemed—and of his relentless quest.

"Have it your way," Hawk said to the Indian.

"Can you move? I have a cabin not far from here."

"No. I not move. I die here. You bury me. Put rocks on top."

Hawk understood. The Crow did not want his body dug up by wolves or coyotes and his gnawed remains flung to the winds. If that happened, what survived would not serve him well in the next world.

"I will do that," Hawk assured him. Looking down at the torn figure, he felt only sadness that he had not been able to save the Crow from the grizzly.

"My woman . . ." the Crow said suddenly, grimacing in pain, his hand clutching tightly at a tuft of grass.

"Where is she?"

Hawk waited for him to reply. Abruptly, the grimace on the Indian's face softened and his hand slowly released the tuft of grass as his torn body gave up the ghost.

Winter was coming on. Hawk had few provisions. Here before him was enough meat to last him a good while. Somehow, despite his wounds, he would have to butcher the elk and the bear and contrive to bring them back to his cabin a good mile from where he now stood. Unfortunately his horse was back in the cabin's corral and he dared not leave these two slaughtered animals untended while he returned for it.

Using his bowie, he ripped his buckskin shirt

into strips, bound up his wounds and his ribs as securely as he could. Then he dragged the dead Indian's body up onto a ridge, covering him with boulders so any marauding coyotes or wolves would not be able to disturb the corpse before Hawk could return with a shovel to bury him properly.

Back at the small clearing, he began the bloody task of butchering the animals. He flung aside the guts and organs for the coyotes and wolves, and as he worked, he kept alert for any more hungry grizzlies. Working as swiftly as he could in spite of his wounds, he soon strapped the choicest portions of the dressed meat onto a make-shift travois fashioned from long pine branches. His Hawken resting on his shoulder and his empty Walker Colt thrust into his belt, he dragged the travois through the timber to the abandoned cabin he had found two weeks earlier. He hung the meat on a hook above the fireplace inside the cabin, mounted his horse, and dragging the bloody travois behind him, rode back in hopes of re-trieving what little meat he had been forced to leave behind.

But before he reached the clearing, he realized he had taken all he was going to from those two carcasses. Still in the timber, he pulled up and watched through the trees as another, smaller griz-zly tore into the elk's remains while two large timber wolves kept a respectful distance. At last the bear left, dragging off the elk's carcass, leav-ing only the dreadfully soiled coat of his fellow

grizzly behind for the wolves. Snarling delightedly, the wolves laced into it, tearing what little
flesh remained.

Hawk rode out of the timber. The wolves
glanced at him. Hawk did not want to shoot
them. He had never tasted the meat of a wolf
and had told himself he would do so only when
he was desperate. One of the wolves took a piece
of the grizzly's matted hide in his mouth and
dragged it off into the timber; the other wolf
followed after him.

By this time Hawk was not feeling too well.
His wounds had broken open—they had never
been completely closed—and the blood oozing
from them was constant. He knew he could not
go on forever bleeding like this. At the same
time, his chest appeared to be on fire. Glancing
up the slope at the spot where he had covered
the dead Indian's body, Hawk wondered whether
it might be wiser for him to forget his promise to
the Indian and ride back as quickly as possible to
the warmth of his cabin.

The fact that he would even consider such a
thing shamed him. Buried deep in Hawk's consciousness was the primitive necessity of seeing
to a decent burial for a fellow warrior, especially
when it meant honoring his dying request. Whether
this need sprang from his white or his Comanche
heritage he had no idea—but it did not matter.
Hawk felt it powerfully, and without further
internal debate, he slid himself carefully off his
horse, pulled free the shovel he had stuck into

his rifle scabbard, and hauled himself wearily up the slope to where he had covered up the Indian. Some of the smaller stones had been dislodged, but there was no sign that the body had been disturbed. Evidently the pungent aroma of the freshly butchered meat below had been too sharp a lure for the wolves.

Slowly, laboriously, Hawk dug the Crow's grave. He was coughing blood almost continually by the time he completed it, and there was a hot, searing pain in his throat—as if he had swallowed scalding coffee. Hawk almost passed out while pulling the stones off the dead Indian so he could drag him into his shallow grave. But he kept to his task doggedly. As he labored, he became aware of the large, soft flakes drifting out of a uniformly gray sky.

At last he uncovered the Indian's body. It had become quite stiff by this time, and Hawk felt a little foolish as he tried to pull the body into the grave. Ants had already come for the feast and some of them left the cold body and began exploring Hawk's torn arm, beginning with his wrist. He dropped the stiff corpse and tried to brush off the swift ants, but was dismayed to see many of them vanishing into his wounds.

Suddenly weak, he sat down heavily and a moment later felt his head strike the ground behind him. He blinked dazedly up at the clouds, feeling his face grow damp from the thousands of large wet snowflakes that blotted out the sky. Dimly, from the bottom of the slope he heard his horse

whinny up at him questioningly. He was thinking of his warm stall in the barn back at the
cabin.

Hawk tried to call out to him, but nothing
came.

The urge to close his eyes for just a minute
was overwhelming. Immediately he drifted off.
When he regained his senses, he was aware of a
shadow moving above him. Another damned grizzly, he thought, grabbing for his Colt and opening
his eyes. Intense black eyes above high cheekbones in a dark, round face were peering down at
him. An Indian woman. At once Hawk remembered that the Crow had mentioned her.

Abruptly, she straightened up and stepped over
him. He turned his head to follow her progress.
She stooped over the Indian's body and with a
quick deftness Hawk envied, she dragged the
stiffened corpse into the grave. Then she took up
the shovel and began filling it, the blade picking
up as much snow as gravel. Then she piled the
wet rocks onto the grave, lugging still heavier boulders onto it.

Finished at last, she slumped down, one arm
draped over the cairn, and began to wail, striking
herself repeatedly and tearing at her hair.

Hawk saw that the woman had no intention of
mutilating herself and that her grief, though obviously genuine, was not entirely overwhelming.
He struggled to a sitting position and waited
until she was done.

At last, deftly braiding the hair she had just

tried to pull from her head, she came over to Hawk. "You hurt bad," the Indian woman told him calmly. She didn't look like a Crow, but she spoke in the Crow tongue.

Hawk's replied in Crow, telling the woman that the same grizzly that had killed her husband had mauled him as well.

She shrugged. "I am not blind. The marks of the grizzly's claws are on you. You die too if I not close your wounds. But my lodge is many moons from here."

"How are you called?"

"They call me Singing Wind."

"I am Hawk."

Again she shrugged. "Singing Wind know this."

"Do you have horse?"

"Yes. The horse of my dead husband."

"My cabin is not far from this place. Help me mount my horse and I will lead you to it."

She reached down, took Hawk's hands, and helped him regain his feet. For a moment, the world spun queasily about him. He felt so light-headed, he wondered why his head didn't spin off his shoulders and vanish into the snow-laden sky.

Seeing his unsteadiness, Singing Wind stayed close beside him, her hand on his back. She was almost as tall as he was, Hawk noticed.

By the time they descended the slope and reached his horse, the snow was half a foot deep, sifting down out of a milk-white sky more thickly with each passing second. There was not the slightest trace of a wind. Singing Wind's horse was tethered close to Hawk's. With one casual heave, she boosted Hawk into his saddle and pushed the shovel into his rifle scabbard, while he groped for the reins. She thrust them impatiently into his hand, then mounted her own horse and looked to him for the direction he had promised.

Head down, he let his mount have its lead, and the horse promptly started through the timber, heading for home.

The cabin's roof was snow-covered by the time they reached it, and night was coming on. The long ride had refreshed him somewhat and the steadily falling snow was like a gentle benediction. It was so silent as they rode through the timber, Hawk swore he could hear the snow falling.

When they reached the cabin, Singing Wind dismounted first, then helped Hawk dismount. He thought he was in fine shape, but when his right foot hit the ground, his knee buckled under him and he fell facedown in the snow. Singing Wind struggled to pull him to his feet, but he rolled over and waved her aside.

"Get my rifle," he told her in Crow. "It's inside the cabin. I'll use it for a crutch."

Hawk struggled to a sitting position in the snow and watched her disappear into the cabin.

He realized he would be in good hands once he made it inside.

A moment later, a tall Comanche strode outside, his forearm locked around Singing Wind's neck, a gleaming blade held under one of her naked breasts. There had been a struggle; Singing Wind's dress had been ripped brutally down the front. She had not let the Comanche take her easily.

Hawk had not had to contend with a Comanche attack for more than a year now, and he had begun to think that the Antelope band—so many leagues south on the Texan high plains—had finally given up on its costly attempt to take his scalp. He saw now how wrong he was. The band's memory of Hawk's betrayal would last as long as the band itself. Hawk barely recognized the Comanche brave, for the last time he had seen him, he had been one of a gang of ten- or twelve-year-olds tearing around the village with others of his size. Hawk now realized that any brave coming of age who was desperate to prove his manhood and take a wife would have to return to the band with Hawk's scalp on his lance. And maybe his balls, too.

"Let her go," Hawk told the brave in harsh Comanche. At the same time he reached back for his stirrup and pulled himself upright. Adrenaline pumped furiously through his weakened body, and Hawk reckoned he still had a chance if the Comanche got close enough.

The Comanche flung Singing Wind aside and

strode toward Hawk. Incredibly, he was carrying a willow coup stick with eagle feathers attached. He had sheathed his knife and in his left hand carried a hatchet with a Spanish broadax blade, a single eagle feather depending from the shaft.

The hollows of the Comanche's cheeks were painted black, signifying the fires of revenge that burned within him, while diagonal streaks of white crossed his forehead; on his naked shoulders broad strokes of blue paint alternated with black, the black predominating. The significance of the paint was not lost on Hawk. The blue symbolized the sky—the habitat of the hawk— while the black signified the hawk's death as an act of retribution. The Comanche was a fearsome, yet magnificent sight as he approached Hawk, and Hawk was sorry that he might have to kill him.

"How are you called?" Hawk demanded, hoping to distract the young warrior.

"Young Eagle," the Comanche replied proudly.

Hawk nodded. It was a name this Comanche had clearly chosen for himself; eagles drove hawks from their hunting grounds, sometimes killing them in the process. That would explain the eagle feather on his hatchet.

"I have just fought the grizzly," Hawk told him. "I am weak from loss of blood. Your victory over me will be a poor one."

"But it will be a victory," the warrior pointed out with a smile—a cruel, vindictive smile that wiped all compassion from Hawk's mind.

Stepping away from his horse, Hawk almost slipped on the snow-slicked ground. Then he took his bowie from its sheath at his side and held it lightly by its tip. The Comanche had heard of Hawk's prowess with a knife. He pulled up warily, his coup stick still held out in front of him, its wavering tip less than a yard from Hawk.

Hawk hurled the large bowie. Expecting this, Young Eagle ducked quickly aside, evading the thrown knife. Triumphant, as if he now had Hawk powerless before him, Young Eagle charged. Hawk's hand flashed back to his sheathed knife behind his neck and sent it flying with lightning speed at Young Eagle. Taken by surprise, Young Eagle did not duck in time and the blade buried itself in his chest.

Staggered, the Comanche glanced down at the knife's protruding hilt, withdrew it, and flung it aside. A gout of blood pulsed from the wound. He looked with fury at Hawk. This second knife he had not expected. Now he was dead, and there was only one thing for him to do. He flung himself toward Hawk, reaching out with his coup stick.

Hawk had expended his last ounce of energy on the last knife throw and was now too weak to even pull back. He felt the coup stick brush against his shoulder as the dying warrior collapsed forward onto him, lashing out feebly with his hatchet. The ax struck Hawk's shoulder, inflicting a painful, but superficial wound. Unable to keep his balance, Hawk collapsed back into the snow, the dying Indian on top of him. With his last remaining surge of energy, Young Eagle raised the hatchet over his head. Dully, bled white by this time, Hawk looked with cold, fatalistic eyes at the hovering ax blade.

It came down, but only crookedly, missing Hawk entirely as a blast from the cabin door tore into the Indian's spine and sent him sprawling off Hawk. The wound in his back and chest turned the snow crimson underneath him. Hawk glanced up and saw Singing Wind standing in the cabin doorway, slowly lowering his Hawken.

Yes, he told himself again, he would be in good hands once he made it safely inside his cabin. Then he passed out.

— 2 —

Hawk didn't know how Singing Wind managed to get him inside, but he awoke not long afterward to find her pulling off his clothes. He tried to say something to her, but it came out in Comanche and that only seemed to startle her. He passed out again and later awoke to a world so quiet it was like a shout in his ears. He glanced out the window and saw nothing, even though he knew it must be close to midday. Singing Wind was over by the fireplace cooking something. The two carcasses he had hung over it were gone, and racks of stripped meat were hanging alongside the fireplace. He frowned. That was a damned lot of meat to strip and cure. How long could he have been out?

Hawk tried to say something to Singing Wind and saw her turn, but it was as if his voice belonged to someone else. For no reason at all his head began to swell and he was terrified that it would crash out through the cabin's roof. Instantly, it seemed, Singing Wind was beside his cot, spooning some evil-smelling potion into his mouth. He fought her off, saw the spoon go flying as she sprang back, her face rippling like a blanket in the wind.

He yelled something at her, but did not hear it, then turned to the wall and fell through it, twisting slowly as he plunged back into darkness.

He was well again. But he was missing something. The fever had burned him out, leaving him as empty as a stove with only ashes left in the potbelly. Singing Wind had to prod open his mouth with her spoon to get any nourishment past his lips. He felt weak, listless. Days passed like fence posts, one no different than the other.

The early-winter storm had long since passed, and Singing Wind, supporting him as best she could, flung open the door one day and helped him outside. He saw the path she had tramped to the barn and noted how high the snow had drifted around the cabin, but it made little impression on him. It was as if he were looking at a painting without color. With Singing Wind supporting him, he hobbled as far as the barn, then returned to the cabin. She led him over to his cot and he fell immediately into a deep, dreamless sleep generated by pure exhaustion.

Singing Wind was patient and persistent. Ev-

ery day after that she forced him to make the
same journey as far as the barn, sometimes getting him to go even farther, following a path she
broke for him. But his exhaustion, both of the
spirit and of the body, was such that all he could
do afterward was sleep. One day she propped
him up on his cot and, using his straight razor
proceeded to shave off his beard. Then she took a
rusty pair of shears she had found somewhere
and began to trim his unruly, tangled mat of long
blond hair. Hawk watched her, feeling nothing,
even though occasionally, as if to arouse him, she
playfully snapped the scissors at him.

He drifted off before she finished trimming
his hair.

It took most of one afternoon to get him into
the washtub and fill it with water hot enough to
scrub him clean. Hawk's wounds were puckered
with scars, he noticed, but the scars were no
longer painful. All the inflammation had gone
down. His elbow was fine and he could flex his
right hand, including the thumb, with little
difficulty—and the deep, boring pain that had
lived in his left side like a small, burrowing
creature, was finally gone.

He leaned his head back against the tub as
Singing Wind washed him all over, leaving no
region untouched. He noted calmly that she was
especially attentive to his groin, but felt no arousal.
He thought he caught a glint of anger in her dark
eyes, but paid no attention. When she helped

him up and dried him off, he went straight to his bed and dropped onto it, asleep the moment his body struck the mattress.

Was he still asleep?

He turned over—or tried to. He couldn't. He opened his eyes and found himself looking deep into Singing Wind's. She was atop him, as naked as he was, her long legs apart, her knees digging into the bed alongside his narrow hips. He felt her hand fumbling with his flaccid penis and groaned, turning his head away from hers.

She plunged her face down and closed her lips about his, her arms enclosing him fiercely as she began to rock back and forth. Hawk was too tired to pull back and let her take him as best she could, dimly aware that it was going well for her and wondering why she bothered. Her tongue slipped past his lips and met his tongue. There was a faint, answering surge deep inside him. He tried to lift his arms to hold her, but could not.

She began to cry out softly to him, murmuring not in her own tongue but in the universal tongue of woman throughout time. Her cries struck an answering note deep within him. As her soft, mewing cries filled his ears, he felt himself stirring. His arms came up off the bed and closed about her slim, silken back, his fingers resting on the indentations of her delicate vertebrae. What happened then he did not know for sure, but a kind of endless roll began, with Singing Wind clasping him so closely he seemed to become part of her flesh.

Hawk drifted off, swimming in a dim tide of warmth and feeling. He felt her lift off his body, then her lips moving hungrily over his face, his neck, his chest, down past his thigh. Everywhere they touched, her lips seared him. Deep within him arousal stirred like a nocturnal beast coming awake to the darkness—and the night's hunt. He felt her back moving like a serpent as she glided up onto him again, her fingers doing what they could to guide him into her. At last her hot, wet moistness folded over him, sucked his growing erection deeply inside her.

Still resting her cheek on his chest, she gasped with delight as she felt him enter her, her crooning sharpening as the teeth of arousal tore at her. Still over him, she lifted up and planted her hands on the bed beside his shoulders as she continued to rock, locked in a dance as universal and unchanging as the stars' march across the heavens. Her hot perspiration struck his face as she leaned over him, and he licked the drops eagerly off his upper lip. Then he felt himself let go, but it was a weak, gasping ejaculation.

An enormous fatigue fell over Hawk. Before he drifted off, he saw the disappointment on Singing Wind's taut face, but he could not help himself as he sank into an exhausted sleep.

He awoke before morning in great distress, his distended shaft throbbing painfully between his thighs. Singing Wind was still in bed with him, tucked against his back, spoonlike, her arms wrapped around his waist. His head clear for the first time in weeks, he trembled with eagerness as he turned swiftly to face Singing Wind, pushed her onto her back, opened her thighs with his knee, then thrust home. She came awake with eyes wide, uttering a small, startled cry. He drove into her with a grim, fierce urgency that would allow no holding back. Swiftly Singing Wind adjusted, flinging her arms about his neck and lifting her buttocks so he could plunge deeper. Half-wild with his urgency, Hawk felt her crossing her ankles behind his back while her long legs scissored his waist.

It was over almost at once for Hawk as he climaxed, but he remained locked within her and was soon able to thrust again, almost as urgently as before, grunting with each thrust. Beneath him, Singing Wind shuddered as he set off a series of minor earthquakes. Over and over, she climaxed, squeezing him tightly with each orgasmic thrust. He lost count of her climaxes, and after two more of his own, he began to regain some control over the wild, naked lust that drove him.

At last they pulled free of each other, both of them covered with fine beads of perspiration. Remembering the disappointment he had seen in her face before he dropped off earlier, he took Singing Wind's face in his big hands and kissed her tenderly on the lips.

"You see," he told her in Crow. "I am still a man. I can satisfy you."

"You are sick no more," she whispered in awe.

It was clear that she had just about given up on him.

"You have cured me. Your warmth has made me alive once more, the feel of your arms about my waist, the fire of your lips. Singing Wind, I think you have just brought me back from the dead."

She smiled then. "Let us be sure. Maybe you are not still dead."

As she spoke, she reached down. Her hot hand closed like a vise about him, and sure enough, he came awake once more. He did not protest, but moved closer to her, holding her tightly and nuzzling her breasts with his lips as she shifted eagerly to greet him.

Hawk did not have any answer as to why he had been so weak all this time and he had no idea how Singing Wind had worked her miracle, but he was well again and she had done it.

They crept closer to the ridge and peered down at the elk herd on its way to the lower valleys where they would spend the winter. There were about sixty in this herd, but most of them were on the far side of the stream, with only a few nearby. One male elk with a massive rack had frozen; his stance was regal as he looked up from the patch of grass his sharp hooves had uncovered a moment before, his nose lifted slightly, testing the wind for sign of predators.

Singing Wind was with Hawk. This was the third herd they had intercepted in the past four weeks, and they had plenty of venison. Hawk had his rifle primed and ready, while Singing Wind preferred her lost warrior husband's bow and arrow. With it, she had already brought down two mule deers.

"Let's get closer," he whispered to her.

She frowned and shook her head at him.

"Come on," he said.

He took her mittened hand and pulled her after him. Again she shook her head. He was about to ask her what the problem was when the snow beneath them gave way and they plunged off the ridge, struck a smooth snowbank, then started rolling down the rest of the slope. The elk was off in an instant, and his warning cry to the herd along the stream was enough to set them all on a run downstream.

As Hawk and Singing Wind sat up in the snow and watched, the last of the elks disappeared beyond an outcropping of spruce. Hawk looked at Singing Wind, feeling faintly ridiculous. She had been trying to warn him that the frozen ridge of snow they had crept out onto was not safe for both of them.

"Singing Wind," he told her, frowning fiercely at her, "why did you not tell me of our danger?"

She shrieked with sudden laughter, picked up a wad of snow, and rubbed his face in it. He howled, blinked away the snow, and did the same to her. She scrambled to her feet in an effort to escape, but he caught her about the waist and brought her down. She turned to face him, her buckskin cloak falling open. Before he knew what he was doing, he had freed one of her breasts and his lips were closing about the nipple.

Singing Wind uttered a cry of delight, sat up, and held his face eagerly to her breast. Hawk moved closer to her and then onto her, the snow packing solidly under them. There was no more laughter then, only a quick, intense need for each other; and under the wide, cloudless blue sky atop a bed of immaculate snow they coupled with the intoxicating joy of wild animals. . . .

They were inside the cabin on a pile of blankets in front of the fireplace. Singing Wind was leaning back into Hawk's arms, and they were letting the fire build within them in order to make its quenching all the more exciting. Singing Wind had just admitted that she was of the Flathead tribe and had been captured by the Crows as a young girl. She had never been happy with the Crow warrior who had purchased her. He had been a poor lover and a miserable provider. His unhappy demise after he brought down the elk was typical of his luck.

Hawk said nothing for a while. Then Singing Wind pushed herself closer to him, turned her head, and gazed mischievously up into his eyes. "When next it comes time for the grizzly to mate," she told him, "we will watch them."

"Singing Wind has seen this?"

"Yes," she answered softly, leaning her head back against his shoulder, "I have seen it."

"Tell me about it."

"Do you want me to? Maybe it is time for you already?" She moved her back into his crotch and wriggled slightly. "I can feel something there."

He grinned at her. "I can hold out as long as you can."

"We shall see." She turned to face him so that she was in his arms, gazing up at him as she spoke. "I was picking berries on a bare slope when a female grizzly came into sight below me. She was grazing farther down and did not see me. Behind her is big male with a fine silver coat. I did not run away. I could see they too busy to notice me. While the female graze, the big male nuzzle her flanks and snuffle in her ears. He groan and pant. He is very anxious. But the female do not pay him much attention. Not at first. But then she not push him away, so the big male is encouraged."

He smiled. "Of course."

"Then another grizzly bear comes. He can smell the female, too. This one is much smaller than the other. The big grizzly turn on him. He chase the younger male away and stand up on his hind legs and bellow. I think he even taller than you."

"Seven feet tall or more. A big one," Hawk commented. "Maybe more than nine hundred pounds."

"Yes. He very big. So the younger male slink off to find himself another female." Singing Wind chuckled as she recalled the scene. "Then the big fellow smell the female and she let him. She is very excited now by all this fuss over her. The big grandfather grizzly sniffle at her with great pleasure, then mount her. She stand rigid until he is inside her. For long, long time the two move little. They are like in a dream.

"At last the female, she get anxious. She back hard into the big one and squirm and wriggle her hips. Like she say, Get going, mister. This awake the big one from his dream of pleasure and he thrust very hard for a while—and then the two are quiet again, until the big one tremble mighty and lunge forward and this time I think he come. His fur ripple all the way up his back. Again and again this happen as the old bear enjoy himself. Then for long time they stay as one. After a while, with the big one still inside her, the female begin to graze like she half-asleep. Sometimes her front legs collapse and she fall softly forward. She too is in a dream. At last, the dream is gone and the big one pull out and nuzzle the female's face. Then they crop the grass side by side and maybe stay together for a week."

"Only a week?"

Singing Wind shrugged, her eyes merry. "I do not know for sure. The female not want this old man around all the time, I think. Only long enough for him to give her cubs."

Gazing into Singing Wind's dark eyes, Hawk took her in his arms and smoothed her long, silken hair—as black as midnight—off her forehead, and began combing it with his fingers.

She reached up and hooked both arms around his neck. "And will you give me cub, too, Hawk?"

The question startled him. He frowned down at her. "Are you with child?"

"Not yet."

He was relieved. A wife and offspring were out of the question for him, and he knew it.

She saw the relief in his eyes and frowned slightly. "Does the Golden Hawk not wish for a manchild?"

"Someday, maybe."

"Is it as they say? You are part bird, part man. That you devour your foes like the Great Cannibal Owl."

He smiled at her. "You saw how I devoured Young Eagle. If you hadn't blown out his backbone, I wouldn't be here with you now."

"Then you are not so terrible, after all."

"I hope not."

"Around the fire at night I hear the braves talk of Golden Hawk like frightened little boys. But I did not believe what they say about you. And I am glad I did not believe it. I would not like for you to change into Great Cannibal Owl while I make love to you."

He laughed. "No chance of that."

"It is your sister you search for, then. This is why you not want a man-child now. Is that not so?"

"It is so."

She nodded, and Hawk could see that his tenacity in continuing his search for his sister only increased her respect for him. "I have heard of your search and that your sister has golden hair. Like you. Is this true?"

He nodded.

"Do you know which tribe has her?"

"The Shoshone. But for a year now, each band I find, they know nothing—or so they say."

"What is your sister called?"

"Annabelle."

"I like for you to find her. But there are many Shoshone bands in these mountains. Still, you must search for her. But perhaps you will never find her."

"I know that, Singing Wind."

She reached up and held her palm against his face lovingly. "Poor man. Poor Great Cannibal Owl."

He held her hand against his face for a moment, then bent to kiss her on the lips. As she returned his kiss and thrust herself eagerly against him, he heard her murmur softly that she would maybe make a little owl with him, if he didn't mind.

There was no more talk as both drank deeply of the other, and at the end of it, she clung to him, sighing softly, and told him to stay in her like the big grizzly. He did, and still coupled, they fell into a deep, dreamless sleep.

The weeks became months. Snows piled upon snows. Sometimes the snow-laden winds that thundered and beat upon the little cabin like some infuriated grizzly seemed strong enough to topple it off its ridge clear into the valley below. Through it all Hawk and Singing Wind slept entwined, oblivious to the storm as they battened to the warmth and security of each other's body, leaving the bed only long enough to eat and keep the fire going.

After each storm would come the awesome silence and they would step out of the cabin to gaze up at the crystal-clear blue skies arching overhead and then squint painfully at the near-blinding fields of shimmering snow spread before them like an immense and immaculate tablecloth. It was unmarred by any tracks and broken only by the islands of timber on the massive flanks of the mountains encircling them. At such times, makeshift sunglasses fashioned of willow twigs tied about their eyes, they would break out of their cabin prison and venture out on the snowshoes Singing Wind had constructed for them. Once they caught a weasel frantically pawing through the snow to get at the mice he could hear tunneling under it. But the pickings were lean, and Singing Wind parceled out what was left of the elk with great care and skill. Hawk had never eaten better in his life, he reflected.

A little after the New Year, after a five-day blow that brought the snow about the cabin almost up to the roof, they set out after a small herd of buffalo moving blindly up the frozen stream, driven this high by the ferocious winds of the past week. All of them were white with snow, their muzzles dripping ice, their massive humps unusually thin, and so weak that they looked ripe for the plucking as they tottered about, their hooves making it doubly difficult for them as they struck the frozen surface of the stream beneath the snow. As Hawk and Singing Wind left the bank and started down the ice toward the small herd, he was thinking of a buffalo robe for himself and perhaps also a buffalo rug for the cabin floor.

There were not more than ten buffalo in all, with a huge old bull in charge. As they approached, the bull moved over and took a stance between them and the rest of the herd. Big though he was, the winter had shrunken him, and there was an air of desperation about him as he lowered his massive head and pawed uncertainly at the ice.

Hawk pulled up; Singing Wind did too. She had her bow and a quiver full of arrows. Hawk had his rifle primed, his powder horn over one shoulder, his bullet pouch over the other. His bowie was in its sheath in his belt; the Walker Colt was back in the cabin, since he had run out of cartridges. Bringing his powder horn to the front in a handier position, he popped two lead balls into his mouth. A third was already in place, its charge of powder secured by a tallow-greased patch firmly seated by the thrust of his hickory rod.

The bull lowered his head and charged. Hawk swung up the Hawken, laid the sights on the chest just under the muzzle, hoping for a lung shot. As he squeezed the trigger, the almost dainty legs of the massive beast slipped out from under him and he went down, the round carrying harmlessly over his head. At once, however, the bull scrambled to his feet and kept coming, gradually building up speed on the treacherous ice.

"Get away, Singing Wind," Hawk cried as he poured powder down the rifle barrel and spat a lead ball after it.

Instead of running off, however, Singing Wind fitted an arrow to her bowstring and swung wide, to catch the charging buffalo in his side, in case Hawk were to miss his next shot. Having no time to argue with her, Hawk rammed home the load and lifted the stock to his shoulder. By then the bull was less than thirty yards away. Sighting this time on the head, Hawk squeezed the trigger.

The Hawken misfired.

Peering anxiously past the acrid smoke, Hawk saw the great humped beast nearly on top of him as one, then two of Singing Wind's arrows slammed into his side. The shafts staggered the bull momentarily, but they had struck nothing vital and slowed the furious brute only slightly. It was too late for Hawk to reload and he no longer trusted the rifle. Spitting out the last ball, he kicked off his snowshoes and dived to his right.

The bull charged past him, trying to hook him with his horn. It took a while for the animal to stop and turn around on the snow-covered ice, and by that time Hawk was on his feet, legging it through the deep snow toward the riverbank. He saw Singing Wind cutting toward him, her bow still held ready.

They both reached the steep riverbank at the same time and found themselves struggling through enormous, overhanging drifts. Hawk glanced back. The bull was bearing down on them with malevolent determination, Singing Wind's two arrows still protruding loosely from his flank. Hawk took Singing Wind by the waist and flung her ahead of him up the embankment; then, holding his rifle's heavy barrel like a club, he turned to face the massive, red-eyed thunderbolt bearing down on him.

Abruptly, a shot rang out from above. The buffalo veered, a steamy gout of blood spurting from his nose. Wobbling under the impact of the bullet, he slipped on the ice and went down, his hind legs kicking feebly. A moment later they were still.

Hawk turned to see who had fired the shot.

A bearded mountain man was standing on the embankment above him, a long-barreled Kentucky rifle in his hands, a curious grin on his face.

"My name's Jim Clyman," he said to Hawk. "And who the hell might you be?"

"Jed Thompson."

"The one they call Golden Hawk?"

Hawk nodded and started up through the drifts after Singing Wind. As he did so, he turned and looked back at the herd to see the remainder of its members moving on up the river, walking carefully, almost delicately on the slippery ice, not a single one of them looking back at the dead bull.

Once on the riverbank, Hawk shook Jim Clyman's hand and thanked him for that shot. Then he introduced the mountain man to Singing Wind.

Clyman looked her up and down approvingly. "Flathead?" he asked her, in a friendly fashion.

She smiled, pleased at Clyman's perceptiveness. "Crows take me captive when I very young."

Clyman looked back at Hawk. "Reckon you two'd be the ones livin' in my cabin."

"Your cabin?"

"Yep. You didn't think God built it, did you? But that's all right. I ain't been in these parts for close on to three years. So you're welcome to it. Looks mighty cozy and I see you patched the roof some."

"It needed it. I chinked up the chimney, too."

"And did a good job, too. You rest up awhile and I'll give you a hand skinning that beast."

"Thanks," Hawk said. "Go on up with Singing Wind then while I go back for my snowshoes." He grinned. "If there are no more buffalo down there, I'll be with you in a minute."

Jim Clyman was already a legend. He had heard about Hawk, but then so had Hawk heard about him—from his friend Bill Williams.

Jim Clyman was not as tall as Hawk, but his bulky frame was solid enough. His face was so completely covered with a black beard that all that showed were his eyes, his rosy cheekbones, his nose, and his broad, tanned forehead. The beard went clear past his Adam's apple, and his hair covered his neck from front to back. He looked like a dangerous wild animal, until you gazed into his great piercing blue eyes. His voice was a soft, pleasant rumble, and as he talked, he filled the cabin with fragrant pipe smoke.

The two men swapped stories far into the night. Only just before it was time to turn in did Jim Clyman mention what had brought him back to this valley and his long-abandoned cabin.

"Pilgrims," he said, shaking his head in disgust. "The more they come, the stupider they get."

"What do you have to do with them?" Hawk asked.

"That's what I'm doin' here in the first place, Hawk. When I passed earlier, I saw smoke comin' from the chimney and knew there was someone living here. I'm mother hen to a flock of white settlers heading for Oregon and the Promised Land. The stupid critters insisted on going through despite the winter snows."

"You couldn't convince them not to?"

"They got themselves a fire-breathin' parson who's in charge of the whole operation. Him and God almighty. He's the one providin' the wagons and provisions, so when he tells his flock to shit, they all squat."

"Where are they now?"

"That's just it. They're about five miles deeper

in the mountains, trapped in Grizzly Pass and nearly out of everything 'cept bibles. They can last another week or so, I figure—if I can keep them from losing their heads.''

Hawk frowned. "There's no tradin' posts nearby. Where could they get fresh provisions?''

"Fort Hall, maybe.''

"How far is it?''

"Two, maybe three days' journey. A week at the most. Will you go, Hawk?''

"Me?''

"I can't go myself. If I leave them poor fools too long, they'll start eating one another. I swear. They're as wild a bunch of fanatics as I ever did see, Hawk. Some are decent, God-fearin' folk, but most of them are red-eyed maniacs, filled with fire and brimstone—closer to the devil than to God, to my way of thinkin'.''

"I'll leave tomorrow. But you got to promise one thing.''

"What's that?''

"Take Singing Wind back to the settlers with you. I don't want her left here alone.''

"Of course.''

Singing Wind had been sitting close to Hawk. Hearing her name mentioned, she glanced with a frown at Hawk. He told her in Crow what he had just asked Jim Clyman to agree too, and why.

"I not need this Jim Clyman to take care of me,'' she told Hawk emphatically.

"Just go with him,'' Hawk urged her.

"Why?''

"Maybe you can help him shoot some fresh game for the settlers."

"No," she told him. "Let him shoot fresh game. When you return, I will be here. I will have fine buffalo robe for you."

Hawk did not like it. The thought of leaving Singing Wind alone in this cabin for any length of time filled him with foreboding. But he did his best to shake off the feeling, for if any woman could take care of herself, Singing Wind could. Hell. She had already saved his life.

Reluctantly, he agreed to let Singing Wind remain in the cabin and wait for his return. Then they bid Jim Clyman good night and retired for the night.

Despite Jim Clyman's presence in the open cabin's far corner, Hawk and Singing Wind made love that night with a passionate intensity Hawk knew he would never forget.

— 3 —

Jim Clyman was at great pains to give Hawk all the directions he would need to get to Fort Hall. And as Hawk passed each landmark Jim mentioned, his admiration for Jim Clyman's knowledge of this rugged high country grew. So as not to exhaust his horse, Hawk alternately rode him, then broke ground for him, resting the animal often and keeping to the ridges as much as possible.

Throughout the first day he trudged across what seemed an interminable landscape of gleaming white snow. He saw no game of any sort, not even tracks. But early in the second day, when he was moving along a long ridge, he caught sight of elk and mule deer spotting a distant mountain flank. Against the naked snowfield, they looked forlorn and vulnerable. But they were well out of range of his Hawken.

Later that same day, as he was breaking a path for his horse through a considerable drift, he caught sight of five Indians riding single-file about a mile ahead of him. They were Bannocks, four of them—a small hunting party from the looks of it. They had two pack horses, one of which was already carrying the dressed carcass of a small elk.

Hawk was not pleased. He knew the Bannocks as a crafty, trecherous tribe that could never really be trusted. Although, like the Shoshone, they boasted of never having killed a white man or harmed a settler passing through their lands, Hawk knew that they were not above welcoming settlers into their encampments and then robbing and killing them all—breaching a tradition of hospitality honored by all Indians, Plains and mountain alike.

Like Hawk, the Bannock party appeared to be heading for the lower valleys. Hawk decided he did not want trouble, so he pulled up and remained where he was until the Bannocks had disappeared beyond a heavy stand of timber. When he set out again, he kept high in the timber, well above the route the Bannocks had taken. He had no desire to mess with this Bannock hunting party. He had another mission, more important than taking Bannock scalps.

And when he was finished, he wanted to return to his cabin . . . and Singing Wind.

That night he camped deep in the timber and ate cold jerky washed down with fresh chunks of snow so as not to risk a fire that might alert the Bannock party. It was a cold night, and when he awoke the next morning, he found himself nearly buried in snow, the trees about him lost in a pale haze as a steady snowfall filtered down through the pines.

Every joint in his body creaked as he stood up, stretched, and shook out his bedroll. The back of his horse was covered with snow, and he did not saddle it until he was positive the animal was as dry and warm as his brush could ensure. Fortunately, Hawk had made it a point to sleep on the saddle blanket. As a result, the blanket was dry and almost warm when he flung it over the horse's back.

Emerging from the pines an hour or so later, he found the snow already beginning to let up as the cloud cover broke apart overhead, revealing large patches of blue sky. By noon Hawk was once again riding across pristine fields of sun-washed snow that grew less deep with each mile he dropped toward the plains. By the end of the day there were only a few scattered patches of snow left. With the towering, snowcapped mountains at his back, the next day he caught sight of the Snake River. Fort Hall, according to Jim Clyman, was only a day and a half's journey farther on down the river, just above the mouth of the Portneuf.

That evening he left the riverbank and entered

a patch of timber to make camp. He shot a rabbit and, for the first time since leaving his cabin, dined on fresh meat washed down with hot coffee. Based on Jim Clyman's directions, Hawk fully expected to reach Fort Hall by nightfall of the following day.

Nearly drunk with exhaustion, the rabbit meat sitting heavily in his stomach, Hawk edged his bedroll closer to his dying campfire and slept.

Dawn broke. Hawk stirred, smelled Indian, and opened his eyes to see an Indian squatting beside him. The Bannock's eyes were glittering with triumph and anticipation. There was even a trace of a smile on his impassive face. Hawk was sick with shame to have been surprised this easily. Three more Bannocks stood back behind the squatting Indian, watching eagerly with gloating black eyes.

Hawk sat up and threw aside his tarp. He saw then that the squatting Bannock was holding his Walker Colt in his right hand, its muzzle leveled on Hawk's gut. Hawk was pleased the Indian had taken the weapon from his saddlebag, since he had long since run out of cartridges. He had been hoping to obtain cartridges for it at the fort. At the moment the big weapon was empty.

Hawk stood up. The Bannock stood up also. Hawk took a step toward him. The startled Bannock took a step back, his three companions doing the same. The Bannock stopped smiling and thumb-cocked the Colt's hammer. He was a mean-looking fellow, with a big nose and a long, grim mouth, and he was surely preparing to blow a hole in Hawk.

But something was holding him back. What that was, Hawk could only guess. Perhaps his fearsome reputation. Whatever it was, Hawk was glad for it and now counted on it.

"What do you want?" Hawk asked.

"Iron Lip want Golden Hawk's scalp," the Bannock replied in rough but passable English. His grim face broke into an exultant smile then—one so wolfish Hawk almost laughed aloud.

"Has Iron Lip not heard of Golden Hawk?"

"Golden Hawk sleep like fool in lap of his enemies. He is a man, not bird. He not fly in air. He not terrible. He snore when he sleep and stink like any white man."

"Reckon you're right at that, chief."

Iron Lips' obsidian eyes became slits. The Bannock leaned closer. He gathered phlegm into his mouth and sent it at Hawk's face. But Hawk had lived long enough among the Comanches to expect this tactic. Ducking easily aside, he let the phlegm snick past his shoulder, then aimed and spat in the Indian's face.

He straightened up and smiled.

The three Indians behind Iron Lips were stunned. Hawk must have powerful medicine indeed to move with such speed and then to show his contempt for their chief in this manner—especially while the Bannock held a cocked revolver inches from his belly.

Trembling with fury, Iron Lips wiped his face. "Does Golden Hawk think I not dare kill him?"

"Hell, chief, You'll kill me." Hawk's smile broadened. "If you can."

At this challenge the Bannock thrust the Colt into Hawk's gut and pulled the trigger. As the hammer clicked down on an empty chamber, Hawk twisted the big Colt out of the astonished Indian's hand and in a slashing, upward motion brought it around against the side of the Bannock's head with such force he cracked the skull.

The crunch of shattered bone filled the early-morning stillness. As Iron Lips crumpled, Hawk reached back for his throwing knife and threw it at the nearest Bannock. The blade sank deep into his throat, in the hollow just below his Adam's apple.

The remaining two Bannocks turned tail and ran. Hawk bent and took his knife from the Bannock's throat, snatched the hatchet from his belt, and then started after the two Bannocks. When he was close enough to one of them, he hurled the hatchet. Its blade crunched through his backbone and sank deep into the Bannock's back just between his shoulder blades. The Bannock stumbled, then crashed to his knees and, still trying to run, plowed facefirst into the ground.

That left one Bannock still alive. Hawk kept after him and was soon close enough to hear the steady pat, pat of the Bannock's moccasins. The terrified Indian, running full out down the broad game trail, looked back. Hawk smiled and drew

still closer. Letting out a keen cry of despair, the
Indian glanced back. By this time it was obvious the Bannock now believed all he had heard
about the Golden Hawk.

Drawing within a few feet of the terrified Bannock, Hawk suddenly ducked to one side and
vanished above him into the timber. Increasing
his speed, he drew abreast of the fleeing Indian
below him, then passed him, his side beginning
to ache and his breath coming in sharp, painful
gasps. Ignoring the discomfort, Hawk plunged
back down through the timber, returned to the
game trail, and headed back up it for a few strides.
Then he caught a low branch and swung up into
a tree over the trail.

Near exhaustion and stumbling in fear and
panic, the Bannock appeared on the trail below. As
he swept under him, Hawk swung down, both feet
striking the staggering Indian on the shoulders,
crushing him to the ground. Hawk chopped his
neck twice with the blade of his hand. The man
went limp. Hawk then slung the Bannock over
his shoulder and clambered back up into the
pine, pulling himself as high as he could get.
Then he sliced off a small scalp lock and wedged
the unconscious Bannock between the tree's limbs
and clambered to the ground. Shading his eyes
from the slanting rays of the morning sun, he
looked back up at the Bannock to make sure he
was still snug.

Hawk was breathing heavily. He was also smiling. He remembered Bill Williams telling why he

had allowed a Blackfoot he had scalped to live. He had wanted the son of a bitch to spread the word that Old Bill was not to be messed with.

It was the same message Hawk wanted to leave as well.

Much later that same day, driving the Bannocks' ponies before him and trailing their pack horses laden with the freshly killed and dressed game, Hawk rode past the blanket Indians clustered about the fort's perimeter and entered the fort. Built by fur trader Nathaniel Wyeth in 1834, it had been sold to the Hudson's Bay Company three years later. The fort was not much to look at, but its walls were high and there were two blockhouses inside the fort and plenty of firing ports in the high walls, not only to fight off unhappy savages, Hawk judged, but to help those inside the fort handle those Indians come to trade who might have sampled too much whiskey before leaving the place.

Hawk headed for the large blockhouse in the far left-hand corner of the fort. On the flagpole in front of it hung the Hudson's Bay Company flag, with its red cross and four rampant beavers. He was halfway to it when a group of mountain men recognized the Indian ponies Hawk was driving. Word passed quickly. Excited shouts were heard all about the enclosed area, and before long, Hawk was surrounded by a horde of mountain men, wide, pleased grins on their faces.

Hawk dismounted as a small man Hawk figured to be the chief trader and head administrator of the Hudson's Bay Company hurried up to greet him officially. He was a seamed, milky-faced gentleman with sleeve garters and a boiled shirt and trousers so tight the bulge between his legs was downright embarrassing ... it was so small. His eyes blinked anxiously as he neared Hawk, and a lock of reddish hair had fallen over his forehead. Pushing through the growing crowd around Hawk, he approached with an outstretched hand.

"Mac Gregor is the name," the little man said, his Scottish burr quite noticeable. "Nate Mac Gregor. On behalf of the Hudson's Bay Company, I welcome you." Then he looked eagerly behind Hawk at the laden pack horses. "And I note with exceeding pleasure the fresh meat you bring us."

"And six Bannock ponies," a mountain man reminded him, grinning like a possum eating yellow jackets.

"Name's Thompson, Jed Thompson," Jed replied.

"Hell, Nate," someone in the back cried. "Don't you know who that is? That's Golden Hawk. He's a friend of Old Bill."

"Any friend of Bill is a friend of mine," said the Scot. "How much do you want for the lot, lad?"

"The ponies?"

"All of them. We can use them for packing."

"Don't forget that fresh meat," another mountain man cried.

"I say we ought to have ourselves a real barbecue," insisted another.

"And then a horse race."

"I didn't come for a horse race," Hawk said to Nate Mac Gregor, speaking loud enough for everyone crowding around to hear. "Jim Clyman and the party he's leadin' to Oregon need help. He sent me here to get it. They need plenty of provisions. His party's trapped in deep snow in Grizzly Pass and they're running out of food."

"Then why in tarnation don't they come back?"

"I told you. They're snowed in. They can't move their wagons."

"Bible-thumpers among them?"

Hawk nodded.

There was a general mutter at that and then a steady buzz of conversation as the mountain men discussed the matter among themselves.

At last one of the mountain men broke from the group and approached Hawk. He was a big man; he stood a good six feet two in moccasins and probably weighed 220. He had large, full pale-blue eyes that appraised Hawk coolly, but with no apparent hostility. A white, puckered scar ran down the right side of his face.

"Grizzly Pass is a far piece from here," he told Hawk. "You think we can make it in time?"

"If we hurry."

"That's not much of an answer."

"It's the best I can do."

"We could get trapped up there ourselves."

"Does that mean you won't help?"

"It don't mean nothing of the sort," he replied sharply. "There ain't a man here wouldn't walk barefoot over the coals of hell to bring Jim Clyman provisions. But that ain't the problem. It's the company he keeps. I'd rather herd chickens than try to guide pilgrims over that high country this time of the year."

"That's right," another mountain man commented. "At least you can eat the chickens when the going gets tough."

"If we don't get provisions to them soon," Hawk said, "they just might get hungry enough to start eating one another."

That seemed to end the discussion.

The mountain men walked with Hawk to the rear of the fort, where he found a stable large enough to accommodate his horse and the Bannock ponies. Mac Gregor left Hawk then, and the big mountain man, who introduced himself to Hawk as Dick Wootton, showed Hawk to his own room alongside the trading post. There, Hawk was shown a tub; he had it filled and took a bath.

Afterward, he joined the barbecue the four Bannocks had provided.

Sitting alongside Wootton on a log while he tore into the shinbone of a young elk, Hawk asked the mountain man about Bill Williams, a mutual friend and fellow trapper.

Wootton sighed and shook his head. "He's gone plumb loco, I figures."

"What do you mean?"

Wootton took out his knife and began picking at his teeth. "Old Bill is now a full-time Ute. He's their big chief and medicine man, from what I hear."

"To the Utes?"

"Yep."

"That don't sound like Bill."

"He was here last summer. I ran into him. He's still got the staggers, but he hits what he aims at. Anyway, he told me the days of the mountain men are done and we might as well go Indian. He said he's already tried going white and that didn't agree with him."

Hawk laughed. In his mind's eye he saw again the raw-boned old reprobate waving him good-bye two years ago, his Indian squaw, Buffalo Flower, standing by his side. He must have abandoned her, Hawk realized with a slight pang. He could feel only affection for the jolly, round Indian woman who had tended him so closely during his fever.

And then Hawk thought of Singing Wind and became uneasy. "How long before we pull out?"

"Tomorrow morning."

"How many are going back with me?"

"There'll be just the two of us. We'll be driving wagons loaded with provisions. Nothin' fancy, you understand, but plenty of grain and other goods, including a few barrels of flour and salt pork. And we'll be leading a string of pack horses in case we get bogged down." Wootton smiled. "We'll be includin' them Bannock ponies you managed to pick up on the way here. Mac Gregor is donating the pack horses and supplies on behalf of the Hudson's Bay Company. Never thought I'd see the day that Scotchman would part with a nickel. Guess he's tryin' to make the HBC look good to us."

"These provisions will look good to the settlers trapped up there with Clyman."

"They will if we make it to them in time."

They were up packing before dawn the next morning and set out just as the first shaft of morning light struck the Hudson's Bay Company's flag whipping in the chill wind. They pushed hard all that day and the next and were soon in snow so deep they had to abandon the wagons and load the pack horses, as they had expected. This took the greater part of a day to accomplish, and when they set out the next morning, they found it hard going. The Bannock ponies did not like being turned into mules, and they put up quite a fuss; but a day later they were resigned to their reduced status and, without setting up a ruckus, plodded along behind the other pack horses through the deepening snow.

Since their route took them within a mile of Hawk's cabin, Hawk left Wootton and cut northwest to it. He was within sight of the cabin when he saw Singing Wind step out the door. She paused in the doorway for a moment, peering steadily in his direction, using her hand as a shade. He pulled up and waved. She waved in turn and ducked back inside the cabin. She reappeared a moment later with her beaver jacket and snowshoes on, and started across the snowfield toward him.

The snow was so deep by this time that Hawk had been forced to dismount and break a path for his horse. Singing Wind met him in the middle of one particularly deep drift. They caught hold of each other and spun about in the snow like two kids, laughing crazily, and for that moment Hawk knew only an incredible warmth as he pulled Singing Wind close to him. At last, with his horse nudging him anxiously, Hawk stood up and brushed himself off, helped Singing Wind brush herself off, then continued on with her to the cabin.

As he stabled the horse, Singing Wind threw fresh logs on the fire. When Hawk entered a moment later, they were thundering in the hearth, sending waves of heat to every corner of the cabin. It was obvious Singing Wind had been waiting for this moment. As soon as he entered, she hurried over to a trunk in the corner. Lifting its lid, she drew forth the buffalo robe she had been working on. She had finished it.

"Take off your clothes," she told him. "Then I see if you like it."

He did not argue with her, especially when she drew close and helped him to accomplish the task. When at last he stood naked before her, she glanced down mischievously and laughed to see what had happened while she was undressing him.

She told him to turn. He did so. Then she lifted the robe onto his shoulders and helped him put it on. He found it surprisingly light. As he tied the sash, he was amazed at how warm and comfortable it was.

"This is a wonderful present, Singing Wind," he said, turning to face her.

"You like it?" Her eyes shone with pleasure as she contemplated him.

"Yes," he said, smiling warmly down at her. "I like it. Very much, Singing Wind. I will wear it always whenever I am in my lodge and the wind howls outside."

She blushed with pleasure at his words. "I am glad you like it. Now you take it off and we make love."

Hawk held the robe open for her. She stepped out of her buckskin dress in an instant, her dark pubic patch already gleaming, then ran to him, pressing herself eagerly against him while he closed the buffalo robe about them both. For a long, delicious moment he crushed her silken, long-limbed body hard against his. Then he opened the robe, lifted her in his arms, and carried her over to the bed.

They ate at midnight, Hawk as famished as a wolf in springtime, after which they slept in each other's arms until dawn. They made love again before getting up. He could not get enough of her incandescent breasts, the eager thrust of her thighs, the feel of her silken arms closing about him. She devoured him with her lips, clinging to him fiercely as they loved like two savages at the dawn of time. There was no history for either of them now—no past, no future—only this full-throated wildness where nothing mattered but their own feverish intent.

They were drunk on each other.

After a huge breakfast, which Hawk ate wearing his new buffalo robe, he dressed and made ready to leave, admonishing her repeatedly to be careful and not to stray too far from the cabin, nor to let anyone close she did not know. He was leaving his Walker Colt with her. At the fort he had obtained paper cartridges and percussion caps for the weapon, and he took pains to show her how to load it. He was not worried about her ability or her willingness to fire the weapon.

Earlier, he had related his encounter with the Bannock hunting party and now he told her to be particularly careful of any Bannocks that happened by, no matter how friendly they might appear.

"Don't trust them," he said. "Those devils might be looking for a way to get even."

Singing Wind laughed. "No Indian would dare harm Golden Hawk's woman."

"Please, Singing Wind," Hawk pleaded gently. "Be serious now."

"All right. I be careful."

She sobered then and he could see in her eyes how much she appreciated his concern for her.

They said good-bye finally, and the hot pressure of her parting kiss was still on his lips, reminding him of her, when he turned in his saddle, waved, and kept on over a snow-capped ridge.

When he looked back again, the cabin was out of sight behind a clump of timber. He felt a sudden strange, sick emptiness, shook it off, then hunched his shoulders and urged his horse along the spine of the ridge where the snow was not so deep, hoping to overtake Dick Wootton by sundown at least.

When he caught sight of Wootton finally, it was late the next day, and the big mountain man was already in sight of Grizzly Pass. The twin peaks hung suspended in the distant sky on either side of the pass like towering nuns, their white habits gleaming against the bright-blue sky. Wootton pulled up when he heard Hawk's shout and seemed glad for the rest. The pack horses were strung out behind him. On a far ridge that ran parallel to Wootton's course, Hawk thought he saw a wolf pack slicing down through the snow.

When Hawk first started to slog through the waist-deep snow toward Wootton, his horse floundering after him, the sky overhead was a bright blue. But by the time he reached Wootton, the black wing of a stormcloud had closed over them, the wind had risen to a shrill, demented scream, and snow was falling. More accurately, it was sweeping horizontally over the landscape, stinging Hawk's eyes, burning his face. Wootton did not try to shout to him above the roar of the wind. Instead, he pointed to a large, concave rock formation on the slope above him that offered some protection from the rising wind, and he started for it.

It was dark before all the horses had been accounted for and were huddling safely in a spot among rocks that offered protection from the storm. The two men built a fire then, constructed a makeshift tent from their tarps, and slowly thawed themselves out. A long, howling night followed.

The only thing they could hear above the wind was the thin, almost plaintive wail of the wolves prowling about in the storm.

Almost as quickly as it had fallen upon them, the storm abated, and by the morning of the next day they moved out. At noon the next day they were close enough to be sighted by Jim Clyman, who had posted himself at the entrance to the pass. With a shout powerful enough to send echoes richocheting around all the snow-covered flanks of the mountains surrounding them, Clyman called out to them. The shout startled Hawk and Wootton, since Clyman was not in sight and all either of them could see in front of them were limitless, sun-drenched fields of snow.

They pulled up, peered into the distance, and saw Clyman at last, waving to them from the crest of a drift piled near the entrance to the pass. They waved back, their lungs sucking painfully on the thin air, and a moment later they saw Clyman leading a contingent of settlers out of the pass to greet them.

When they got close enough, Hawk noted at once that those with Jim were mostly women and children—and a more pitifully gaunt collection of pilgrims Hawk hoped never to see again. Nevertheless, as they neared Hawk and Wootton and saw the long train of pack horses loaded down with goods, they shouted themselves hoarse and rushed past Hawk and Wootton to the long line of pack horses strung out for a quarter-mile behind them.

A disturbingly thin Jim Clyman shook Hawk's hand, then Wootton's.

"I knew you'd make it, Hawk," Jim said. Then to Wootton he said, "And thanks, Dick, for comin' along."

"Wouldn't have missed it."

"How bad has it been?" Hawk asked.

"Bad enough. I told you it would be close. Right this minute I figure we got enough food for another day maybe, but we've been on short rations for the past week and we're all pretty weak. We sure cut it close, I can tell you."

There was nothing more to say as Hawk,

Wootton, and Jim Clyman continued on to the pass, the women and children following eagerly with the pack horses.

The settlers' wagons had been stopped cold in the middle of the pass, with only their snow-covered canvas tops still visible above the deep drifts packed about them. In between and around the wagons, burrowed deep into the snowdrifts were the rounded, tunneled-out shelters of the settlers.

"Well, now," Hawk said to Clyman, "these here snow houses look snug enough."

As he and Wootton passed by one, Hawk glanced in and saw where pieces of furniture had been set up inside them; a small fire was going, the smoke from it passing out through a small hole in the top of the domed shelter.

"Mebbe so, Hawk. But it's damned hard to keep warm inside them. It's like livin' inside a block of ice. It was twenty below last night and every one of us felt it. We've stripped what firewood we could from the mountain flanks around us, but there just ain't enough left."

"You mean there are not enough able-bodied men willing to go get it," Hawk said.

Clyman nodded in sullen agreement. "That's about the size of it, Hawk. How'd you figure that?"

"I got eyes," he said, glancing around him.

While most of the women were busy unloading the horses and carting away the provisions, he could see others busy laying out laundry on the bright, sun-kissed snowfields around the wagons, their faces raw from the constant wind and terrible cold. Other women and children could be seen lugging buckets of snow over to fires to melt for water. On all sides Hawk saw women and young children laboring at various tasks while the cruel wind tugged at them.

Yet not a single man had stepped out of the shelters to lend a hand. They were keeping inside, well out of the reach of the harsh winds, perfectly content to allow their women and children to unload the horses and store the goods—in short, to take care of everything for them. The men of this wagon train were, as usual, a crop of useless, ne'er-do-well failures from the East. What amazed Hawk was the willingness of their women to go along with their men on these fool journeys into the wilderness.

Hawk looked at Jim Clyman. "It's time to get the men off their asses. I say we bring them out to help the women unload the pack horses."

"Just what I been thinking," seconded Wootton.

"Who's their leader?" Hawk asked.

"Reverend Amos Twitchell. But I warn you, Hawk, he don't take advice easy."

"I don't give a pinch of coon shit how he takes advice."

"You want me to go get him, then?"

Hawk nodded decisively. "And if he gives you any shit, don't be easy on him."

A broad smile on his face, Clyman ducked

quickly into one of the largest of the snow shelters. A second later came the sound of angry voices. Then Clyman appeared, dragging the reverend out of his shelter by the nape of his neck. As the man twisted angrily in Clyman's grasp, Jim nudged him roughly over to Hawk. Meanwhile, all work in the camp ceased as the women and children held up eagerly to watch. Behind Twitchell the wagon train's male complement appeared in front of their shelters, heavy blankets wrapped around them as they looked on.

"Be you the Reverend Twitchell?" Hawk asked him.

"Yes," the man said, pulling himself up to his full height as he tried to get his outraged thoughts in order. "And just who might you be?"

"Someone who's come a long ways to beat your ass to a pulp, that's who."

At Hawk's words, many of the women shrank back in shock. But a surprisingly large contingent elbowed one another eagerly and grinned happily at their parson's comedown. The children were wide-eyed with wonder at the sight of their preacher being handled in such a fashion.

"Sir! How dare you," cried the reverend.

"How dare *you* lead women and children into these mountains at this time of the year? Reverend, you must be mad to do such a thing! If a single one of them dies, it'll be on your soul!"

Twitchell paled and shrank back. Dressed only in thin black cotton trousers and a shirt, he was an incredibly lank, bony fellow with a long blade of a nose and close-set, watery blue eyes. His cheeks were sunken, hollow, his chin bony and receding. His scrawny neck was punctuated by an enormous Adam's apple that bobbed now in apprehension and outrage.

"Who gives you the right to speak to me in this fashion? And by what right do you come here and threaten a man of God and his flock!"

"Hell, Parson," Jim Clyman said angrily, "Hawk here's the one who just saved your bacon. He's the one brought your people provisions. He's the one saved them. Him and Dick Wootton. Not you and not God. If you live through this, you'll have them two to thank for it."

"Get some warm clothes on, Reverend," advised Hawk, a mean smile cracking his grim face, "you and the rest of your male flock."

The preacher frowned warily. "Why, sir, what do you intend?"

"I intend for you to start chopping up these here wagons for firewood."

"You must be mad! They'll be needed when spring comes. They will afford us transportation to Oregon."

"Sorry, Reverend, but you won't be seeing Oregon this spring."

"That's absurd!"

"Stay here in this pass and you won't see spring anywhere. Now start chopping up the wagons for firewood. Right now your people need warmth and a chance to regain their strength if they're going to make it back safely to Fort Hall."

"Fort Hall?"

"You heard me, Reverend."

The reverend was aghast at this change in his plans. "Why . . . I tell you, I won't have it! Who put you in charge of this wagon train?"

Hawk looked at Jim Clyman. "Was it you, Jim?"

Jim laughed. "Guess mebbe it was at that, Hawk."

"I think you and Mr. Clyman are mad," the reverend said, incensed. "We will treat your interference with the contempt it deserves. The Lord Himself will see us all safely to Oregon—with or without your interference! We will chop up no wagons and make no plans whatsoever for retreating to Fort Hall."

Hawk stepped forward, took the reverend by his shirt collar, spun him about, then lifted him above his head. The fellow seemed no more substantial than a bundle of kindling as he screamed and began to kick wildly. With an easy heave, Hawk flung him into a snowbank. The reverend hit head and shoulders first, and broke through the snow. Only his backside and legs were visible as he struggled to extricate himself. Flopping about wildly, his mouth clogged with snow, he got to his feet and turned on Hawk, his face livid, his entire body quivering with rage and indignation.

Dick Wootton took a step toward Twitchell. "No more delay, Reverend," he warned, "or we'll have you chopping up those wagons with your pants off."

The reverend stared at Wootton in dismay. "Why . . . why, I do believe you mean that!"

"You bet your frozen ass I do."

Twitchell looked helplessly about him. The women had been delighted a second before to see him pitched headlong into the snowbank. Now they were watching him coldly, offering him no encouragement in his attempt to defy Jim—and the men crouching outside their shelters seemed even less willing to go to the reverend's aid.

One of them cleared his throat nervously. "Looks like we ain't got no choice, Reverend."

That did it. The reverend saw the handwriting on the wall.

He turned and ducked back into his shelter, the rest of his male congregation disappearing just as hastily into their own shelters to get properly dressed for what lay ahead.

Seeing this and knowing they would soon be leaving this frigid pass, the women and children began talking excitedly among themsleves. Not a single one of them seemed in the least unhappy at this change in their plans. Indeed, more than a few of the women gazed fondly at the three men, assuming they were responsible. One woman in particular—a tall, rawboned, auburn-haired beauty—seemed to have singled Hawk out from the other two men, and the instant her hazel eyes met Hawk's, she smiled at him with a warmth so tangible that Hawk felt strangely moved.

Still talking together excitedly about this abrupt

change in their plans, the women and children hurried off.

Jim Clyman turned and grinned widely at Hawk. "Damned if this ain't the happiest day of my life!"

Hawk shrugged. "Chopping up these wagons for firewood is only half of it. Getting these pilgrims the hell out of here and back to Fort Hall is the other half. And that won't be so easy."

Wootton spoke up then. "It'll be tough, sure enough. But we've brought them the provisions to make it. Besides, what choice do they have? There's no way they can last through the winter up here. There's the rest of January and all of February to go yet. This pass won't be clear until May or June."

Jim Clyman spoke up wearily. "That's what I been tellin' that crazy bible-thumper."

"So we move out as soon as we can," Hawk told him.

"Done."

A sudden peal of thunder cracked over their heads. Hawk glanced up and saw a thunderbolt rip down from a swift-moving black cloud and bury itself in a huge drift high above the camp. A great spray of snow was flung up. Another lightning bolt followed the first, and then came a tremendous, continuous roll of thunder, like an infinite number of war drums pounding in unison.

Snow, sudden and stinging, swept down from the black cloud that now completely shut out the blue sky of a few moments before. A sharp, knifelike blast of cold air struck Hawk, and as the lightning and thunder continued to play about them, Hawk followed Jim Clyman and Dick Wootton into a shelter that had been shoveled out behind one of the wagons.

Hawk cursed. It was not going to be as easy as he had thought to get these pilgrims back down out of Grizzly Pass.

— 4 —

Three days later the snow was still falling, a steady, blinding snowfall, whipped by fierce winds. With astonishing speed the snow built up, soon covering the wagons completely. The men had had no chance to chop them up as Hawk had ordered, and the wagons were rediscovered by the settlers, who found shelter in them once more, the snow drifting over their canvas-covered frames offering excellent protection against the wind.

On the fourth night it was still snowing, and that was when the wolves arrived.

Four-year-old Amy Smythe dropped down from her wagon, bundled so snugly she looked like a fur muff fitted with tiny arms and legs. The sound of a dog close by had caused her to leave her small cot. It was almost daylight. The snow had let up some and she could see the dog just ahead of her now on the well-packed snow trail, the same one who had only a moment before poked his muzzle through the canvas opening and then peered down at her, his sharp ears alert.

In Illinois she had had a big furry dog for a companion. It had yellow fur and used to follow her around, protecting her. Sometimes Amy would curl up against its side and fall asleep. Its name was Boy, and her mother and father had decided not to take it with them on the trip west. Too much trouble, her father had told her when she asked him.

Amy could see the dog waiting for her. She ran toward him.

"Here, Boy," she piped eagerly.

The pack leader froze, its hackles lifted. The man smell was on this one and every instinct told him to flee. But another instinct, more basic— the same one that had brought him down into this curious settlement and caused him to peer in at the sleeping forms in the wagon—now caused the big male wolf to lower its head and peel its lips back off its fangs, uttering a deep, low, terrible growl.

Amy Smythe had never been growled at like this before. Boy never growled at her—only at those who came too close or seemed threatening. She pulled to a halt, less than a foot from the wolf, and cautiously extended her hand to pet him. She remembered how eagerly Boy would thrust his head closer and lift it under her hand so that she could pet it, his tail wagging happily all the while.

But this dog did not wag his tail and made no effort to place his head under her extended palm. Instead, it crouched lower, the growl deep in his throat becoming more frightening. A sharp note of alarm sounded deep within Amy and she pulled her hand back quickly, fear suddenly constricting her throat.

She would have turned and run if the wolf, unable to control his ravenous hunger any longer, had not sprung. His powerful jaws snapped down on Amy's neck, crunching through the spine. Amy felt nothing. She was dead instantly. The huge gray wolf, holding the bloody bundle easily between his teeth, leapt up onto the snow embankment lining the passageway between the wagons, then dug up the steep slope toward a small patch of scrub pine still showing above the drifts.

Before he reached the pine, the rest of his pack bounded out of it to join him. Tongues lolling, they danced around the big wolf as he dropped his prey to the snow between his front paws and began to snap and gnaw at the tiny arms and legs. One small gray male wolf, barely three years old, ventured close, but a warning bark from the big wolf was enough to send the foolish youngster back on his heels. There was no doubt who would feast on this prize.

And there was no doubt, either, where other

morsels such as this one could be found. In the gray light of morning, the snow still casting a dim pall over the pass, the rest of the wolf pack left its leader and swept down the slopes toward the cluster of snow-covered wagons below.

Not much later, fierce and brazen in their hunger, the wolves were discovered prowling among the wagons. An outcry was raised at once. Hawk, his rifle in hand, saw one of them leaping over a wagon. He took after him at once, his boots a little unsteady on the ice-encrusted paths that ran between the wagons. Wootton and Clyman were right on his heels.

Then Hawk saw another at the far end of the wagons, leaping after his companion. And then another. They were on the run now that the alarm had been sounded. These were huge gray fellows, the same wolves, Hawk surmised, that he and Wootton had heard prowling about on their way to Grizzly Pass. The wolves had sounded hungry then; they must be famished now. Nothing less than starvation could bring them this far into human habitation.

A scream—a woman's high, terrified scream—cut through the interminable keening of the wind. Hawk stopped and spun in its direction.

"Now, what?" Wootton muttered. He was eager to get after the two wolves he had just seen.

"Trouble, sure enough," said Jim Clyman.

Then came an angry, agonizing shout from one of the men. "Reverend," he cried. "Reverend! My little girl! She's gone!"

Cursing, Hawk clambered out of the narrow pathway up onto the snowbanks and cut across the snow toward the sound of the woman's screams. More than once his feet broke through the new snow and he was forced to fight his way on through the drifts. When at last he reached the wailing, grief-stricken woman, she was surrounded by most of the camp's settlers. Beside her, down on one knee, was her husband, a pale, narrow-featured fellow, his eyes closed now in supplication as he clasped his hands and prayed to heaven that what appeared to have happened had not happened.

Hawk alighted beside the mother. The women pulled back to give him room. Gently, Hawk shook the woman until she stopped screaming and focused her eyes on him.

"When's the last time you saw your girl?" Hawk asked.

"She was asleep beside me. But when I woke she was gone."

"How old is she? What's her name?"

"She's only four. Her name's Amy."

Hawk nodded. He remembered the little girl now. A cute, curious little settler with big hazel eyes. His heart went cold as he thought of her in the jaws of one of these famished wolves.

Jim Clyman stepped closer. "Did she have any friends she might have gone to see?"

"Yes! And at first I thought that's where she went. But she wasn't at their wagon. I've searched everywhere! And now these wolves . . ."

Through all this, the father of Amy Smythe continued his despairing supplication of the almighty. Rushing up, then kneeling beside him in the snow, came Reverend Twitchell, his prayer book clasped in his hands. At a wave from him, the rest of the settlers crowding around dropped to their knees to join him in prayer.

Before the little girl's mother could follow the others, Hawk took her by the arm. "Where's your wagon?"

She pointed.

Hawk hurried to it, Clyman and Wootton at his side. The snow had covered any tracks the little girl might have left, but when they followed the path leading from the rear of her wagon, they saw at once the break in the embankment where the wolf had leapt up onto it with his tiny burden. Brushing aside the light cover of snow, they found the few frozen droplets of Amy's blood.

From there the wolf's trail led straight up the slope, the slight indentation in the snow left by his passage not yet covered by the falling snow. The three men peered up at the tops of the scrub pine sticking out of the windswept snowfields at least half a mile above them.

"He's up there," Hawk noted grimly.

"Think she's alive?" asked Wootton.

"Not a chance," said Jim Clyman. "She was dead the moment the wolf took her. Remember, there was no outcry."

Hawk looked over the rest of the snowfield.

"There's no sign those wolves we just saw have retreated any. Go back and warn those bible-thumpers, Jim. Tell them to get their firearms. These wolves are hungry."

"Where you goin'?"

"After that wolf who took the girl."

"Need any help?" Wootton asked.

"No. Just get these settlers off their knees. That's a hell of a place to be with a hungry wolf staring into your face."

Three-quarters of the way up the slope, Hawk caught sight of the wolf. He was in plain sight, about a hundred yards or so below the scrub pine, nuzzling frantically at something in the snow. As Hawk watched, the animal's jaws closed about a small bundle of blood and sinew and he shook it back and forth fiercely in an effort to get at what was left of the tightly wrapped remains of Amy Smythe.

Hawk dropped flat and popped two lead balls into his mouth. Grabbing his powder horn, he poured it in, dropped a third lead ball in with his tallow-greased patch, and with his hickory rod seated the load home. Once the load was seated firmly, he peered up at the wolf. The still-famished wolf was worrying Amy Smythe's remains.

Hawk crept forward cautiously, keeping his head down and holding his Hawken inches above the snow. The wolf was too busy to notice him, and with the heavy snow hanging like a gauze curtain between him and the animal and the stiff wind carrying Hawk's scent back down the slope, Hawk was able to get to within 150 yards of the wolf before holding up. The wolf was still doing his best to rip apart the thick swaddling that remained wrapped about Amy's corpse.

The rifle fired in almost flat trajectory over distances up to 150 yards. In shooting matches at Fort Union a year or so back, Hawk had been able to shoot a branch out from under a blackbird at close to 200 yards without harming the bird. And with the slow twist of the Hawken's rifling, there was almost no recoil. It was a sweet rifle his father—through Two Horns—had willed him, and he was grateful for it.

Hawk rested the sight on the chest of the wolf as the wolf suddenly paused to stare down the slope through the swirling curtain of snow. The animal appeared to be looking straight at him. Hawk stood up quickly, aimed, and squeezed off his shot in one swift, fluid movement. The wolf was already darting to one side as the half-ounce ball of lead smashed him high in the shoulder instead of the chest, knocking him back over his tail.

Hawk got to his feet and struggled up the remainder of the slope, pouring powder down his rifle barrel as he ran, then ramming home one of the two balls he had popped into his mouth earlier. The wolf was lying on its side, quivering. What remained of Amy lay beside the animal in the snow: a pitifully torn fragment of clothing and blood, pieces of white, cracked bone protruding from it in spots.

The sight made Hawk's stomach turn.

Within a few yards of the wolf, Hawk pulled up and aimed down at the animal, astonished at the wolf's powerful build and enormous length. From behind him he heard a sharp, low growl and the panting struggle of another wolf charging up the slope toward him. He turned and saw a smaller, leaner wolf coming at him—undoubtedly this big one's mate.

Wolves mate for life, Hawk knew. A female wolf will fight to the death for her cubs. She will fight almost as hard for her mate, and despite the snow's depth, this wolf was hurtling toward Hawk like a streak of white fury, her eyes red, her tongue lolling as she closed in on him.

Hawk lifted the crescent-shaped butt of the rifle to his shoulder and fired point-blank at the onrushing wolf, knowing that he could not miss. The lead ball caught the female squarely in the chest, ripping through its white ruff and seeming to crush the animal into the snow like a giant, invisible fist.

A deep growl from behind alerted Hawk. He turned as the downed male, his powerful torso dark with his own blood, leapt upon him. His snarling jaws snapping furiously, his forepaws heavy on his shoulders, the wolf sent Hawk tumbling back in the snow, the thrusting, insensate face of the animal inches from his own as he held him off. Beneath Hawk a drift gave way and he began to slip sideways back down the slope, the enraged, snarling wolf still atop him. As he unsheathed his bowie, Hawk thrust his well-covered left forearm into the wolf's slavering jaw to hold him off.

The drift gave way beneath Hawk and both he and the wolf plunged a few feet farther down the slope. Hawk wrapped his thighs around the wolf and plunged his knife into the spot where the animal's spine joined his head. Uttering a pitiful cry, the wolf shuddered from head to tail, but he did not let go of Hawk's forearm. With the wolf's snarling visage still inches from his own throat, Hawk kept on plunging the bowie's long blade into the big wolf until he realized at last he was only butchering a corpse.

Hawk had to work some to get his forearm free of the wolf's jaw. When he did so, he found that despite his heavy sleeve and the woolen shirt beneath it, the enraged wolf's teeth had managed to sink deep into his arm in more than a few places. The lacerations looked ugly, and much of the skin was torn. The arm was already heavy with blood.

Hawk got to his feet and trudged back up the slope through the snow to retrieve his rifle. Not wishing the parents of Amy Smythe to see what was left of their daughter, he picked up her remains and tossed them as far as he could into the scrub pine. Though by this time the snow had let up completely, Hawk knew that more snow was inevitable and would soon cover Amy's mangled corpse.

He turned and started back down into the pass.

More than halfway down the slope, Hawk heard screams and shouting from the camp below, followed by a rattle of rifle fire. Coming to a halt, he glimpsed what was left of the wolf pack racing away from the wagons, heading on through the pass. And he saw something else as well: a body being dragged by a large white wolf who was just able to keep himself ahead of his fellow wolves. They were in clear view, racing across an open snowfield. One wolf, then another was dropped by those firing from the wagons, but the new leader of the wolf pack clung to his grisly prize and disappeared from sight, his pack right on his heels.

"Who was it?" Hawk asked as he approached Jim Clyman.

Jim was standing on top of one of the snow-covered wagons. It was the highest spot in the camp, affording him an excellent view of the pass. He jumped down beside Hawk and glanced at him grimly.

"It was the Reverend Amos Twitchell."

"How'd it happen?"

Clyman shook his head. "Damnedest thing I ever saw."

Wootton joined them. He had heard Hawk's question. "The reverend gave his life for one of the children," he said.

"He did what?"

"We were off chasing a couple of big ones down the other side of the wagons," Jim Clyman explained. "We had told the women and children to stay in the wagons."

"A five-year-old boy who'd been looking out the rear of his wagon spotted the big white wolf," Wootton continued. "He had a broomstick in his hand and was shooting at it when the wolf leapt up and dragged the kid out of the wagon."

"That didn't look like any five-year-old I saw from above."

"It wasn't a five-year-old," said Jim Clyman.

Wootton said, "It was the reverend."

"How did that happen?"

"The reverend came running when he heard the screams, and attacked the wolf with a shovel."

"A shovel?"

"That's right. He broke the handle and then tried to beat the wolf with the stump. The wolf dropped the kid and leapt on the reverend. By the time we got there, the wolf was streaking off, holding the reverend by the nape of his neck. He was as limp as a rag doll, and we knew he was dead."

"How's the kid?"

"Got some nasty bites. I figure he'll carry one scar on his face clear to the grave." Wootton shook his head grimly. "Teach him not to shoot at wolves with broomsticks."

Jim Clyman sighed and looked around, then

up at the sky. "Anyone notice," he said. "The snow's let up."

"We can get out of here," agreed a weary Dick Wootton.

"Just what I was thinking too," said Hawk.

"How soon do we move out?"

"What's wrong with tomorrow?"

"Not a thing. Not a damn thing."

Hawk looked in the direction the wolf pack had taken. Those wolves had served a grim purpose, he realized. There would no longer be much opposition for pulling out and heading for Fort Hall.

At the same time Hawk realized he had underestimated the Reverend Amos Twitchell. A biblethumper he had been, a distinct annoyance, and perhaps even a fool.

But he had died to save the life of one of his flock.

Hawk was leaning against one of the wagons an hour or so later, examining the lacerations left by the wolf's teeth, when he heard a sharp intake of breath behind him. He turned to see the auburn-haired woman he had noticed earlier staring at his bleeding forearm. By this time he knew her name: Alice Gentry.

"How did that happen?" she demanded.

"The wolf I went after."

"The wolf that killed Amy Smythe?"

"Yes."

"But you mentioned nothing at all about your wounds. They need care."

"I reckon they do."

"Come to my wagon."

He wanted to say no. Since the first time he had noticed Alice Gentry—or rather had felt the warmth of her smile—he had made every effort to avoid her. He felt silly doing this; more than once she had passed him, smiling at him as she had before, but each time he pretended not to see her. At last she had given up acknowledging his presence as well. This had been what he wanted; Singing Wind was enough for him.

Yet the moment Alice Gentry stopped noticing him, Hawk began thinking of her. She was the only woman in the wagon train without a husband, and she remained aloof from most of the camp's activities. She owned land in Oregon, and it was whispered around the camp that she was intent on opening a business there as soon as she reached Oregon City. The kind of business she was planning on opening was also a matter of whispers.

Hawk had paid no heed to the rumors, and was intent now only on stopping the steady flow of blood from his torn-up forearm. He knew the loss of blood could cause him a lot of trouble, and the trip back down this mountain to Fort Hall was not going to be an easy one.

"I'd be grateful," Hawk said, "if you'd help me stop the bleeding. What I need are some fresh bandages, I guess."

Once they reached her wagon, Alice pushed him gently down into a soft chair piled with pillows. Her bed was neatly made and was snugly placed against the chair. With the snow covering the canvas top entirely, there was little light, only what filtered through the snow cover and what came in through the rear of the wagon. The place was surprisingly warm, however—perhaps too warm—and it was filled with the smell of Alice Gentry.

"We'll have to do more than stop the flow of blood, Mr. Hawk," she told him.

"You can call me Jed," he told her.

"You mean you really do have a Christian name?"

He just nodded, wondering at her sarcasm. Saying nothing more, she took off his coat and shirt, stripping him bare to the waist. Then she tore some sheets into strips and wound them tightly about his wounds to stop the bleeding. When she had done this, he thanked her and was about to leave when she stopped him with a firm hand on his chest.

"You sit right there, Jed. I'm going to have to melt some snow and then boil it. I'm not done with you yet."

When she came back with the pot of boiling water, she dropped some of the torn sheets into it, unwound the bandages from around his forearm, and began scrubbing the wounds clean. Hawk had never felt such pain, but he contented him-

self with staring grimly into Alice Gentry's hazel
eyes.

After a while he lay back, his forearm numb by
this time, perspiration oozing out of every pore.
Once Alice had cleaned out the lacerations and
bound his forearm as tightly as before, she
wrapped chunks of ice and snow with pieces of
torn bedsheets and held the ice against his arm.
The painful throbbing eased almost at once, and
after a while there was very little pain left.

He opened his eyes in wonderment at this treatment and found himself looking deeply into her
hazel eyes.

She blushed at the intentness of his gaze. "Does
that feel better?"

"It sure does."

"My father was a physician. In Boston. When I
get to Oregon City I am going to open up a clinic.
I will be able to treat people then as they should
be treated, without recourse to bleeding and other
cruel medications."

"I heard you were on your way to Oregon City.
And I know you were going to open a business."

She snorted contemptuously. "And I am fully
aware of the kind of business I was supposed to
be opening. These fools! They are so busy talking
about evil because they are so completely fasci-
nated by it. I think they would be very bad if they
had the courage."

She was so close to him that he could smell the
sweet perfume of her breath as she spoke. With
his good arm, he reached up and pulled her lips

down onto his. In a moment they were working hungrily, eagerly. He left the chair and rolled her over onto her bed. She did not protest. Her free hand swiftly unlaced her bodice and she pulled out her breasts for him. He closed his lips hungrily about first one nipple, then the other. He drank deeply of her, wanting more. Under him, she swelled voluptuously, and he heard her groan, then begin to protest.

"Stop complaining," he told her sharply. "You know this is what you want!"

"Yes, Jed! Yes! It's what I've wanted since I first saw you!"

"Shut up now and let me have you!"

She nodded dutifully, and with her hand resting on the back of his head, she pressed his mouth down upon her heaving breast while he yanked furiously on her skirts.

"Tear them," she muttered. "Rip them!"

He did as she told him, the sound adding to the excitement he felt as his groin quickened almost painfully. Then there were only her silk, frilly underpants. He grabbed them by the waist and tore them off her, took one of her hip bones, and shoved her brutally underneath him. Lifting just once, he plunged eagerly into her and felt her engulf him gratefully, both her arms quickening about his neck.

Gasping softly, she began thrusting upward to meet every one of his downthrusts, keeping in savage unison with him until they were both unaware of anything else in the universe. With an incredible rush, he climaxed, his fists pounding into the pillow beside her head, while she moaned loudly and flung her head wildly from side to side—and he felt her come also, her juices flowing out copiously from around his shaft.

Breathing heavily, he pushed himself up onto his hands, then kissed her hard, brutally hard, on the lips. He was thinking of Singing Wind and hating himself and wanting this woman beneath him again—and soon.

"Oh, my," Alice gasped, attempting to smile, "that was really something. It was like mating with part of the wilderness itself."

"Now, what's that supposed to mean?"

She felt his anger and was puzzled by it. But she said only, "I am sorry, Jed. I don't know what I meant. Forgive me." Her arms tightened about his neck. "Again," she whispered fiercely, her eyes like pools he wanted to lose himself in forever, her lithe body upthrusting hungrily, urgently against his. "Please, Jed. Again. That was so impossibly sweet."

"It was good, all right," he muttered.

She reached down and pulled his erection upright, then lifted herself so expertly that he was inside her once again. He felt her vaginal muscles close eagerly about him and began thrusting. His anger was gone now—along with any more thoughts of Singing Wind. He was caught up in the wild excitement of making love in a universe so close, so shut off from the rest of the world that it seemed this feverish moment was all there was or ever would be.

Before he reached his climax, Alice pushed him onto his back and then swung over on top of him. "It's better for me this way," she explained eagerly. "I can get you in so deep."

He didn't argue.

She blew a lock of wet auburn hair out of her eyes and promptly went wild. Leaning swiftly back and with a violence he was afraid would hurt her, she drove herself down onto his erection. Gasping with pleasure, she began to pound on his chest, then started to ride him—twisting and plunging, first forward, then sideways, gyrating around and around, working her pelvis furiously. He was amazed and delighted at her moves. They did wonders for him as well as he gazed up at her, occasionally grabbing one of her breasts and hanging on.

She began to explode then, repeatedly, each time letting out a cry that sounded like a sob. He felt her gushing and it became tricky staying inside her. At last, unable to keep himself from climaxing any longer, he let himself go. Reaching up and pulling her to him convulsively, he pulsed wildly up into her, grunting fiercely with each throbbing ejaculation. She laughed deeply, delightedly, and pulled him closer to her, tightening her vaginal muscles about his shaft in a fierce, determined effort to keep him erect.

It worked.

Laughing excitedly, she began to move once more—steadily, slowly this time. His shaft probed so deeply at times that its tip seemed to him to be on fire. Still thrusting gently, she leaned away suddenly and began to sing softly, happily. He reached up and ran his long fingers through her thick auburn hair. She laughed and, still singing softly, leaned closer, throwing her long, damp auburn hair over him, so close that he could take one of her nipples in his mouth and suck on it. Her soft singing became a low moan then, and he found himself coming alive, lifting to meet her thrust for thrust, the gathering ache in his groin becoming intolerable.

Suddenly he reached out and grabbed her narrow hips and swung her around under him in one swift motion. She gasped up at him in surprise as he prowled over her, then proceeded to slam down into her repeatedly, with a fierceness that caused jagged little cries of pleasure to break from her slack mouth. He was through playing. His urgency allowed for no more gentleness as he raced brutally toward his climax.

When it came, it caused her to respond just as powerfully, and for a long moment the two emptied themselves into each other, clinging together with the closeness of vines, gasping, laughing softly—covered all over with fine beads of perspiration.

Hawk leaned back and closed his eyes. Alice leaned close enough for him to catch one of her nipples in his mouth. He closed his lips about it and drifted off, aware of the fetid perfume of her body enclosing him. He awoke once, aware of her still holding him, looked past her at the pale canvas roof—at the sunlight filtering in through the snow cover—and then dropped off again.

When he awoke, it was dark and he realized he had slept through the day. He was still in the bed, naked under the sheets, and Alice was dressing his arm by the light of a coal oil lamp. A concerned face looked into the wagon through the round opening in the rear. Hawk recognized Dick Wootton.

"How is he?" Dick asked.

"Better," Alice said. "Much better."

"We're moving out tomorrow."

"Move out, then. He can't be moved. I think the wounds are infected."

"We'll wait, then."

"Another day. Give us another day."

Wootton nodded. His face vanished from the opening.

Alice was lying. Hawk knew how a wound felt when it was healing properly—slightly itchy—and that was exactly how his forearm felt. But even though he knew she was lying, he said nothing as he turned to look up at her.

She smiled down at him, finished tying the bandage, then blew out the lamp. In a moment she was out of her nightgown, had thrown back the sheets, and her long, hot limbs were pressed hard against him. He grabbed her fiercely and closed his lips over hers.

He was caught up, he realized, in a hunger for Alice and her body that went to the very roots of his soul, filling him with a need wild and inchoate. It was dangerous, he felt dimly, and strangely debilitating to lust after any woman this badly, yet there was nothing he could do to pull himself back from this obsession.

And even worse, there was nothing he wanted to do.

— 5 —

The journey back from Grizzly Pass proceeded with surprising ease. The settlers had lost only two wagons to firewood and the rest, they knew, would be waiting for them, come spring. Meanwhile, the snow had let up and a January thaw had set in, easing the cold if not the footing. Most of the women and children rode the horses that had drawn the wagons and the pack horses Hawk had brought with him. The men willingly broke the trail on foot where that was necessary.

They were within a few miles of Jim Clyman's cabin when Hawk saw Jim waiting by the trail for him. Hawk knew what Jim was going to suggest, and it filled him with immediate, irrational resentment. Behind him on his horse sat Alice Gentry, her arms tucked snugly about his middle, her cheek resting against the small of his back. She felt remarkably comfortable back there.

Jim Clyman reached up to take the halter on Hawk's horse.

Hawk pulled up. "What is it, Jim?"

"Just a reminder," he said. "You could cut off here if you want. The cabin's not far. You've done enough for these pilgrims—more than enough—and I thank you."

"That's all right, Jim. I'm going all the way to Fort Hall."

"That so?" Jim wasn't surprised, though he tried to act as if he were. He was a poor actor.

"I promised Alice."

Jim's glance at Alice was a cold one. He nodded and stepped back.

Hawk urged his horse on and did not look back at Jim or up at the pines on the slope above, beyond which was the trail he could have taken back to the cabin . . . and Singing Wind.

He felt Alice's arms tightening affectionately about his waist and heard her murmur of thanks for keeping his promise to her. He said nothing and kept his thoughts away from the cabin, thinking only of the end of their trek through this white wilderness and of a time when he could be completely alone once more with Alice Gentry.

The arrival of the settlers at Fort Hall was a time for rejoicing, both for Mac Gregor and the mountain men and other settlers wintering there. The gaunt, weary settlers were greeted with hot food and warm lodging and the promise of a safe, if uneventful, stopover until winter had finished with this stretch of the divide. That they had made it back safely was all that mattered, and the settlers immediately held a service to give thanks, with a solemn but eloquent young lad leading them instead of the late Reverend Twitchell.

Alice, it turned out, was a woman of considerable means. Keeping herself apart from the rest of the settlers, she rented quarters from Mac Gregor that were far from the grainery or the cook shack, and there she and Hawk retreated, ignoring the scrape of the fiddle and the shouts of the caller as the square dancing commenced.

On the trail down from the pass, Hawk and Alice had slept close by each other, but prudence had kept them apart. Now, it was as if the doors of a pent-up furnace had been suddenly flung open. They could not get at each other quickly enough. They tore into each other like hungry birds at carrion. She told him she wanted him to rip her clothes from her and he had done so gladly, the sound of her ripping garments throwing fuel on the fire that consumed him.

Then she had fastened to him like a leech, sucking him and holding him and taking him deeper and still deeper—until both cried out at the end of it like wild animals and collapsed, thoroughly spent, into each other's arms. Hawk felt her trying to arouse him just once more, but he pushed her away groggily, turned his head, and slept deeply.

When he awoke, still sprawled in her arms, he found the fiddle and the foot-stomping had stopped entirely, along with the cries of laughter and the happy shouts of the men sampling Mac Gregor's whiskey stores. The fort was still—as still as death.

He got up carefully so as not to disturb Alice and went to the window and looked out at the fort's moonlit quadrangle and the gate beyond. Not a soul was in sight. He felt suddenly very lonely.

"Hawk . . . ?"

He turned. Alice was sitting up in bed.

"I'm over here," he told her.

She left the bed and padded to his side on naked feet, a tall, willowy wraith of a woman, with long auburn tresses that coiled about her shoulders and her breasts, some of the curls entwining her nipples. Her patch gleamed mysteriously in the darkness.

She moved against him, the feel of her nakedness against his inflaming him. He draped one arm about her shoulder.

"It is so quiet," she said, as if reading his thoughts.

"Yes."

"And just look at that moon."

"I'll be going back to my cabin tomorrow," he told her suddenly, his voice hoarse.

"But why?"

"I have things to get."

"What things?"

"Never mind what things," he told her roughly. "I have to go back up there."

His voice brooked no argument. It was as if a steel door had slammed down the moment she asked the question. She did not argue with him. He looked away from her and back up at the huge silvery moon. He had not once mentioned to Alice anything about Singing Wind, and he never would. Singing Wind was something special and apart. And now he had to go back to her. He regretted not having left the settlers on the way here when Jim had suggested it.

Alice snaked her hand up about his neck. She turned him slightly and leaned gently against him. Then her lips found his. There was no angry, furious passion now. That particular storm had passed. Instead, something new blossomed between them, something more deadly—a tenderness coupled with raw desire.

He found himself unable to hold back. Her mouth opened and her tongue moved out like a serpent to scorch his lips and set fire to his loins. She felt him come alive against her and laughed softy, seductively. Without a word, his desire for her choking in his throat, Hawk took her up in his arms and carried her back to the bed.

There was no more talk of him going back to his cabin that night—or during the nights that followed.

*   *   *

The same moon that shone over Fort Hall that night was noticed by Singing Wind. Restless, she stood at the window, looking out upon the moonlit stretch of snow-covered meadowland that extended down from the ridge. For too many days she had waited for Hawk's footprints to break that clean expanse as he moved up the ridge to the cabin.

What she felt, she did not tell even herself. But until a week before, she had strapped on her snowshoes and gone hunting every day, going as far as the trail she knew Hawk had taken on his way up to Grizzly Pass. She knew how long it should have taken him to bring the provisions to the settlers, and now she waited anxiously for his return. It seemed that he had been gone a very long time.

And then, one bright day, with the sun glancing brightly off the snow, she had seen the settlers retreating from Grizzly Pass, the women riding the horses, most of the men on foot breaking the way for them. She had been on the edge of a clump of juniper when she first caught sight of them. Hurrying to its edge, she peered down at the long, streaming file of settlers, looking eagerly for sign of Hawk.

When she caught sight of him at last, he was on his horse, a white woman sitting behind him, her arms tight about his waist.

Singing Wind had felt a quick stab of dismay, then immediately thought better of it. It did not matter what her eyes told her. Singing Wind was

Hawk's woman. Hawk was only helping one of the settlers. It was obvious where they were going. Back to the fort. And that was a good idea. Only insane whites would try to haul their wagons through Grizzly Pass in the middle of winter.

And as soon as they reached the fort, Hawk would return to her. After all, he had left his new buffalo robe behind, the one she had just made for him. He would not want to lose that. She wiped away the tears that came unbidden, turned, and made her way back to the cabin. From that day on, she had not gone hunting again, content to nibble on the little jerky still left from the buffalo while she waited for Hawk's return.

When, she wondered dully, would he return? Would he ever return? The question was too much for her. Her heart beating queerly, she left the window and went to her bed. But she did not sleep.

Sick of jerky, a week later Singing Wind left the cabin and went in search of fresh game. She moved swiftly, effortlessly on her snowshoes, and though she had the Walker Colt Hawk had given her stuck into her belt, she relied on her bow and arrow.

The Crows had always chided her for practicing so often with a bow and arrow, but after her marriage they no longer said a word. They knew that if the two of them were to live, it would be as much by her efforts as by those of her inept husband. Then had come Golden Hawk. Like a spirit from the wood, he was—and kind and strong. With his long rifle she did not need her bow and arrow. And what pleasure he gave a woman!

Now, once again she was having to rely on her own prowess with a bow and arrow, and perhaps that was best. After almost two hours she caught sight of movement ahead of her in a clump of pine and headed for it. By the time she reached it, she saw the tail of a mule deer retreating. She kicked off her snowshoes and raced through the stand of pine. When she reached its far side, she saw the deer in the middle of a clearing, pausing in its flight to test the wind.

Singing Wind sent an arrow into its side. The animal leapt, ran a few yards, then slowed. She hurried out after it and sent a second shaft into it, this one burying itself in the deer's neck. The deer moved off quickly to the right, jumped once, pathetically, then collapsed facedown into the snow.

Jubilant, Singing Wind advanced on the deer and proceeded to butcher it, not failing to notice how poorly it dressed. It had been a long winter already for this scrawny creature, she realized. But now, at least, Singing Wind would have fresh stew for Hawk when he returned.

The haunches thrown over her neck, what she had cut and dressed dragging behind her in a leather sack, Singing Wind made her way back to the cabin. It was close to sundown when she caught sight of the cabin on the ridge below her.

And then she saw the footprints of a man leading his horse up the slope to the ridge, and then his footprints going from the barn to the cabin. Hawk had returned as she knew he would! Still dragging the sack of dressed meat behind her in the snow, she hurried on down the slope to the cabin. Outside the cabin she left the meat and burst jubilantly through the door.

A tall Comanche warrior was standing in the middle of the room. His face was painted with considerable skill. He gazed coldly at her and smiled grimly. She spun around. Four Bannocks, each as hideously painted as the Comanche, entered the cabin behind her. One of them had lost part of his scalp.

She shrank close to the wall.

The Comanche approached her. "Where is Golden Hawk?" he asked in miserable Crow.

Singing Wind remembered then her foolish response when Hawk had warned her not to wander too far from the cabin. It was not true that no Indian would dare harm Golden Hawk's woman. She grabbed for the big gun Hawk had given her. The Comanche struck it from her grasp, then slapped her so hard that she trembled all over and slumped back against the wall.

Again the Comanche asked, "Where is Golden Hawk?"

Singing Wind closed her mouth firmly. She would say nothing. She was Golden Hawk's woman and would do nothing that would dishonor him.

Hawk's uneasiness would not let him sleep. As silent as a shadow, he left his bed without disturbing Alice, dressed swiftly, and let himself out onto the fort's quadrangle. The wind had died down and the stars were winking brightly in the night sky. It was the silence that awakened him, he realized.

He saw a light in the sutler's grog shop and plowed through the deep snow toward it. He found Jim Clyman inside, nursing a whiskey at a table in the rear. Jim waved him over. Hawk slumped at Clyman's table. Without a word the sutler came over with a mug for Hawk, and Jim filled it with his bottle. Jim, too, was silent.

It was the lateness of the hour, perhaps, or the sudden, blessed silence from the interminable wind.

Despite the fact that it was past midnight, the sutler was still going over his inventory. That day, despite the storm, a load of supplies had come in, the last shipment Mac Gregor could count on until spring, the teamster told him. This came as no surprise to anyone, including Mac Gregor. Fort Hall had been lucky so far; the snow had been light all winter, the mountains getting hit the hardest.

But this past week had made up for it.

"Can't sleep?" Hawk asked, and he downed most of the whiskey.

"Yep. Makes the silence kind of loud, don't it? But I've been waiting for this."

"Pulling out?"

"Yep," Jim said.

"When?"

"First thing in the morning. That roan I bought is all packed. I'll be riding the black when I pull out. Can't see spendin' the rest of the winter in this place. It ain't Mac Gregor. He's sure been decent. It's all these bible-thumpin' pilgrims. They smell worse'n a stable."

Hawk nodded. He felt the same way, and as he listened to Jim Clyman, he found himself envying the man.

"Which direction you taking?"

"I won't be going back to the cabin, if that's what you're thinkin'."

Yes. That was what Hawk had been thinking—and the moment he thought of Singing Wind, it felt as though he'd been kicked in the stomach. But he said nothing and just shrugged.

"I'll be going beyond Grizzly Pass," Jim went on. "When I was up there, searching for fresh meat, I found me a hidden valley with a lake and a river pouring out of it filled with beaver. And other game, too. Maybe I'll get me a little squaw and stay up there for a while. Get the stench of white folks out of my nostrils."

Hawk grinned at him suddenly. "You wouldn't want to give me any hint of where I could find that valley, would you?"

"Hell, no."

"Didn't think so. Hidden pretty well, is it?"

"You'd never think it was there if you didn't know it. I was chasing a whitetail when I came on it."

Hawk leaned back and sipped his whiskey. For a moment he considered asking Jim to stop by the cabin on his way and say good-bye to Singing Wind for him. Since Jim was going toward Grizzly Pass, it would not be much out of his way. And he had just mentioned that he would like to find himself a squaw. Singing Wind would do Jim nicely.

But Hawk could not get the words out. And the thought of Jim taking Singing Wind with him to his valley set the blood pounding in his temples angrily—as if it had already happened. In that instant he realized why he had been unable to sleep, why the sudden silence had sent him from Alice's bed into the starlit night. He was remembering the days and nights he had spent with Singing Wind while those fierce snow squalls howled about the cabin—and then the awesome, wondrous silences that followed, as if the whole world had been made over again and was waiting for them to step out into it and make the first tracks.

He pushed his mug over for more whiskey. As soon as Jim filled the mug, Hawk downed it. The whiskey smote him like a fist and all doubt vanished. He saw his way clear.

"Guess maybe I'll be pulling out with you, then," he told Jim. "As far as the cabin anyway."

"Tomorrow morning?"

"Yes."

"That's pretty short notice, ain't it?"

"I've got the rest of the night to get my gear ready," Hawk said.

"I'll be welcoming your company, Hawk, but what of your woman? You and her been pretty close these past weeks."

"That's my business, Jim, and I'll thank you not to concern yourself with it. Now, do you want my company or not?"

"I already told you, Hawk. I'll be welcoming it, and I'll remember to keep my fool mouth shut, too. That I will."

The raw whiskey burning a hole in his stomach, Hawk got up, left the sutler's, and returned to Alice Gentry's quarters—and her bedroom. A lamp on her nightstand was lit and she was sitting up in bed with her back against the headboard. When Hawk entered the room, she was combing out her auburn hair, and when he saw this, he wondered if all women knew as much or had the powers that Alice Gentry possessed.

"You left quietly, but I heard you go," she said. "I wondered what kept you."

"The storm is passed finally. The stars are out."

"Oh! You went out to see the stars, did you?"

"That was part of it." He wondered why she enjoyed making him feel foolish at times—why she seemed to need to get the advantage over him, as if they were in some kind of contest.

"Only part of it? And what was the other reason?"

"I was thirsty for a drink," he said, lying deliberately, knowing the answer would unsettle her.

He saw the alarm in her eyes and knew he had accomplished his purpose and was glad. Then he said, "I am going back to the cabin. I think you'll be safe here at the fort, come spring."

"The cabin?"

"Yes."

"Oh, Jed. Must we go over that ground again? What is there up there in that cabin that can't wait until spring?"

Hawk still had said nothing to her about Singing Wind, but he knew that Alice suspected something. Perhaps Jim Clyman or Dick Wootton had spoken to Mac Gregor or one of the settlers and it had gotten back to Alice. But he didn't care. He would say nothing to Alice about Singing Wind, and this time he would not stay here with Alice.

It was very simple. He did not belong here.

"Come to bed, darling," she said, smiling up at him. She put down her brush and held her arms out to him.

He felt himself being pulled toward her. She moved closer. The blanket fell away, exposing her breasts, and he felt his mouth go dry. But he turned away and headed over to the big steamer trunk against the far wall where he had stowed most of his gear.

"I'm leaving tomorrow morning," he told her. "I'd better get my things ready."

For a long moment there was no sound from Alice.

"Let me help," she said cheerfully enough, no trace of irritation or anger in her voice. "We don't have all that much time, do we?"

He had reached the trunk. He turned to look back at her. She was on her feet, tying the sash on her robe, no anger in her face. As her eyes caught his, she smiled warmly.

Hawk breathed a deep sigh of relief. She was not going to be difficult. For that, he told himself, he would always remember Alice Gentry fondly.

Hawk and Jim Clyman set out the next morning. They made good time for a day, but then more snow, sweeping down from the north, delayed them, almost turning them back to Fort Hall. But they kept on, and Jim left Hawk a few miles from the cabin and headed northwest into high country, where snow appeared to be a permanent curtain over the mountain peaks. Not long afterward, trudging through a bright, clear day, Hawk found himself cutting across familiar country once again and knew the cabin was not far.

His heart ached now. Not with sorrow, but joy. Glancing around him at the wild country, the awesome, lonely beauty of the peaks, and the snow-covered mountain flanks, he knew this was where he belonged. Singing Wind was his woman, and soon he would be with her, wrapped in that snug buffalo robe she had made for him.

It was a few hours before dusk when he caught sight of the cabin, still a tiny, snug bastion amid towering drifts. Struggling through the deep snow, leading his horse, he stopped suddenly and peered with a frown at the cabin. The door was open and no smoke came from the chimney. Tired of waiting for his return, Singing Wind must have left and gone back to her people!

Filled with dismay at his loss, Hawk charged up the remainder of the slope and burst through the open door. But Singing Wind had not left. Spread-eagled on his robe, what remained of her torn, naked body pierced by lances, she was still waiting for him. He found himself staring at her open mouth and imagined he could hear the cry that must have come from it at the end. He knew without being told that she had called out for him.

He stepped forward and gently removed each lance. Four Bannock lances and one Comanche lance. He flung aside the lances and knelt beside Singing Wind, cradling her head in his arms, rocking mindlessly back and forth until the awful, bottomless grief within him boiled away, leaving only a seething desire to find and punish those responsible.

He stepped outside to the white, pristine world, turned his face to the sky, and cried out his vengeance—a long cry of inchoate fury that broke from the darkest hollows of his soul. It came back to him in a series of rolling echoes, and somewhere an overhanging drift of snow loosened and crashed down a mountainside, its rumble dying away only slowly.

Hawk turned and went back inside to Singing Wind.

— 6 —

Jim Clyman's valley was not hard for Hawk to find, given the clues Jim had let drop and remembering the direction Jim had taken when he parted from Hawk. Jim had not exaggerated the valley's isolation and beauty. Its sides were almost sheer, with forested ridges on top and no apparent way down to the stream threading through it, now blanketed with snow-covered ice. Nevertheless, Hawk kept going, leading his horse ever farther along the treacherous, snow-laden ridges, until at last he came upon a game trail that dropped through the steep, timbered slopes. Two days later he gained the valley floor and saw ahead of him a large snow-covered pond gleaming in the noonday sun.

It took another day for Hawk to find Jim Clyman. The big mountain man was in the process of raising a small cabin and seemed more than a little perturbed by Hawk's presence—until he caught the grim cast to his face as Hawk rode toward him. Driving the blade of his ax into a log he was trimming, Jim came to meet Hawk.

"Nice valley you got here, Jim."

"That it is."

"Sorry to break into it like this."

"What is it, Hawk?"

"It's Singing Wind," Hawk told Jim quietly. "She's dead."

"How did it happen?"

"Four Bannocks and a Comanche. They left their lances."

"Calling cards?"

Hawk nodded.

"The Comanche—is he from that band in Texas that's still after you?"

Hawk nodded. "Must be."

"And the Bannocks?"

"They got a score to settle with me, so they joined up with this Comanche, looks like."

"You goin' after them?"

Hawk nodded.

"And you want me to go with you?"

"Just after the Bannocks, Jim. The Comanche I'll take care of, if I have to track him clear through hell."

"Light and rest a spell. We'll pull out come mornin'. I been gettin' a mite weary of building a cabin all by my lonesome anyway."

Hawk swung out of his saddle and led his

horse over to Jim's crude lean-to close by the stream. He was pleased at the sight of the fresh beaver tail hanging on a spit over the fire. Having not eaten much this past week, he was ravenous.

He had been feeding on hate instead.

Their horses a full mile behind them, Hawk and Jim Clyman inched their way through the timber to the ridge overlooking the Bannock winter encampment. It was on a level plain at the head of a broad valley. The snow did not appear very deep, and a sizable pony herd was grazing deeper up the valley. The ponies' sharp hooves had long since cut through the snow cover, enabling them to graze on the short buffalo grass. Between the lodges, racks were covered with strips of buffalo or deer meat drying in the sun.

"From the looks of it, they been having a fine winter," said Jim Clyman.

Hawk nodded grimly. "Well, maybe we can put an end to that."

The two men had already settled on what they would do when they came upon the Bannock encampment: nothing. Not until Hawk was able to spot the Bannock whose scalp he had partly removed earlier. It would take a while, both men realized, and they would just have to be patient.

"A mean bunch, these here Bannocks," Jim Clyman muttered. "They was the only redskins Ashley would never trade with—not less'n he had a steady bead on 'em."

"Let's get closer."

With a shrug, the big mountain man followed Hawk down through the timber. Hawk pulled up within less than a hundred yards of the nearest Bannock lodge, leaving them both still safely covered.

"This is close enough," Hawk said. "We'll watch from here."

"You're damn right it's close, Hawk. Gives me the creeping willies. We better keep an eye out for their dogs."

"We won't find that son of a bitch 'less we can see him," Hawk reminded Jim.

The mountain man shrugged. He could not argue with that fact, and he began making a rough bedding on the pines needles a few inches under the snow. Before long, the two men had provided a somewhat cramped den for themselves, one that was effectively screened from the Bannock village by snow-laden pines and juniper. It would be a cold camp and more than likely a long one, but they dared not show themselves or do anything that might draw attention to their presence.

The Bannock would love to find them. In one late-night discussion with Hawk and Dick Wootton, Mac Gregor had insisted that the Bannocks were not only heathen, but cannibals as well, and even worse rumors and accusations concerning the tribe had long circulated in these mountains.

But none of this mattered to Hawk as he settled down to watch the comings and goings of the Bannock tribesmen and women. All Hawk needed was one glimpse of that Bannock, a part of whose scalp he had taken. He could not be certain that he had been party to the murder of Singing Wind—or even that he belonged to this particular band. But it was good place to begin, the only real chance Hawk had to find those four Bannocks who had left their lances in Singing Wind's body.

He knew where to find the wielder of the Comanche lance, and if he had to return to the Staked Plains and his old Comanche brothers to find him, Hawk would do so.

But first things first: those four Bannocks.

Three days later, sooner than either Hawk or Jim had expected, the partially scalped Bannock and three fellow warriors rode into the village a few hours before sunset, driving before them the small herd of ponies they had stolen. The village erupted immediately, and a great celebration ensued, the drums beating constantly while the returning warriors danced their victory dance and filled the night with their unashamed boasting. Remembering similar celebrations during his years with the Comanches, Hawk was glad no captives had been brought back along with the stolen ponies. The captives would have been turned over to the women and the night would have come alive with the stark and terrible screams of the tormented and dying.

Meanwhile, Hawk and Jim had noticed that all

four of the returning Bannock warriors were without their lances.

In the week that followed both men watched the four Bannocks closely. The Bannock Hawk had partially scalped, they called Scalped. One of the other three had a dark, scowling face and wore a heavy bear-claw necklace around his neck; his jaw was unusually prominent, so Hawk decided to call him Big Jaw. The remaining two were Red Paint and Little Swagger, because of the former's fondness for painting his face red and the latter for his short, stumpy stature and the strutting way he walked.

The four Bannocks remained in the village for a week. They were content to bask in the glory of their exploits, holding court to the younger braves and accepting visits from the older men of the tribe, all of whom were eager to share in the warriors' glory. Jim and Hawk had to wait for any one of the four Bannocks to move out of the protection of the village, and it was a long week for them. Their quarters were cramped and the nights turned very cold indeed as the January thaw became a February freeze that reached into their bone marrow.

Meanwhile, during this long vigil, their view of the village was such that they came to understand much of what went on within it; they became virtual participants in its daily activities and in the lives of some of its inhabitants. More than once the two men saw braves slipping into the lodges of their young lady friends or stealing off into the timber with them for greater privacy. And the winter's long, brutal cold caused the death of two old ones, a warrior who left many lamenting relatives, and a toothless, homeless old woman without kin who died at last huddled in a ragged blanket against the outside skirt of a lodge in a desperate but futile effort to gain some heat.

The night was dark, the wind high, its chill chasing the Bannocks into their lodges early, and so Hawk had dared a fire, being extremely careful to let it burn cleanly without sending any smoke into the air. The two men had long since dug a deep hearth in the ground to ensure that any light from their fire would not be seen from the village.

Glancing sidelong at Hawk, Jim drawled, "Dammit, I'm getting to know these people too well. It'll be like murdering family if we have to open up on any of them."

Hawk pulled his blanket more closely about his shoulders and leaned closer to the tiny fire, holding his mittened hands out over it. Without looking at Jim, he nodded gloomily. He felt almost the same way. These days had brought back the memory of the many years he had spent in the village of the Comanches who had captured him when he was only fourteen. There was not really all that much difference between the two peoples—at least not from this distance.

Despite their fierce savagery in battle and their reputation for treachery, among their own people the Bannocks appeared to be a kind and considerate band. They were filled with merriment and good cheer, despite the miserable cold and the growing scarcity of food as hunters returned without fresh game. Every day both men witnessed many instances of kindness, and they came to recognize and like a few of the children as they watched them play on the snow-covered river that coiled around their village.

"It doesn't make any difference how we feel," Hawk told Jim grimly. "Those four are dead Indians. If you want to pull out, Jim, I won't stop you. You've done more than any other man would do, and I won't soon forget you for this."

"Shut up, hoss," said Jim gruffly. "I never said nothin' about pullin' out. I just said it won't be easy if we have to open up on these redskins. But I reckon if the time came, I could manage it well enough."

Hawk nodded.

The time came two days later.

Early in the morning, Little Swagger and two older warriors rode out to hunt for fresh game. In an excess of optimism they were leading two pack horses. The night before, a young brave had returned to the village with news of an elk herd nearby. But evidently only Little Swagger and the two moving out with him had decided that the young brave's sighting was reliable enough to warrant a hunting party.

Watching them go, Hawk told Jim, "Stay here and keep an eye on those other three. I won't be long."

"Hell with that, Hawk. I'm comin' too."

Hawk shrugged and did not argue as he climbed out of their camp's narrow confines, stretched himself like a large cat, then set out for the distant hollow where they were keeping their own mounts.

Late that same day, crouching in a clump of birch over a narrow valley, Hawk and Jim watched the three Indians riding slowly toward them. Beyond the ridge ahead of the Indians, both men knew, grazed a small herd of elk, gaunt from lack of food and worn out from the long winter. Whatever Little Swagger's hunting party managed to kill would hardly be worth carrying back to the village, but the three Indians did not know this. They would be grateful for what little meat these winter-gaunted elks could provide.

It was only Little Swagger that Hawk wanted. Hawk had taken the trouble to bring along one of the four lances he had taken from Singing Wind's body. It did not matter whether the one he had brought with him belonged to Little Swagger. Scalp and the others would have no difficulty recognizing the lance or understanding its meaning when Hawk left it behind.

The three Indians came at the small elk herd from three sides, driving the animals up the steep slope before them. Hip-deep, the snow was enough to stop the fleeing herd in its tracks. Firing their flintlocks calmly into the frantic animals and loosing their arrows with deadly effect, the hunters brought down five of the fattest elks, then proceeded to dress them and load up their pack horses, ignoring the thin line of wolves that materialized on the ridge above. It was dusk before their task was completed, and in a small clump of pine below the lip of a protective ridge, the weary Bannocks made camp for the night.

Waiting until midnight and the light of a cold, bright moon, Hawk and Jim at last moved down through the pines until they reached the Bannocks' camp. Moving through the snow like a great white snake, Hawk burrowed close to the three Bannocks, Jim close behind him. It was his job to see to it that Hawk was not disturbed when he singled out Little Swagger.

At a signal from Hawk, Jim stood up and positioned himself over the three sleeping Bannocks, his back to a tree, his revolver cocked and ready. Snow chilled Hawk's wrists and some of it found its way down the back of his buckskin shirt as he burrowed the remaining distance to Little Swagger's blanketed form. Pulling to a halt beside the Indian, Hawk clapped his left hand over his mouth and plunged his bowie hilt-deep into the Indian's chest. Astonishingly, the Bannock came fully awake in an instant and shot bolt upright. Hawk slammed him back down into the snow, where the Bannock trembled violently for a few seconds, then was still.

The disturbance was enough to cause the two other Indians to stir slightly. But they did not come fully awake. Hawk waited until he was certain they were sound asleep once more, then looped a rope over Little Swagger's neck and dragged him slowly into the protection of the pines. That accomplished, he slung the dead Bannock over his shoulder and climbed one of the pines. Hawk attached the rope to a branch and let Little Swagger drop. Standing under him a moment later, Hawk let fly the lance he had brought with him. The lance's iron tip plunged into the chest wound Hawk had inflicted, driving the body back. Hawk ducked aside as the rope's grisly burden swung past him.

A moment later, as he and Jim moved away, Hawk glanced back and saw Little Swagger's body twisting slowly, his head tilted awkwardly to one side, the lance protruding from his chest. Hawk felt some satisfaction, but not much.

There were still three more to go—not counting the Comanche.

Well before dawn a great black cloud obliterated the moon. With it came a knife edge of cold, a cruel wind, and snow. It was falling steadily when the next day broke. Watching from the ridge, the two men saw the remaining Bannocks searching for their missing comrade and heard their cries when he was found. Not long afterward, the Bannocks set out through the driving snow with their grisly burden slung over one of the pack horses. One of the riders carried the lance Hawk had left, and as the two Bannocks rode off, they cast fearful glances about them. Death had visited their camp while they slept but had let them live. It was enough to send a chill up each of their spines.

When the two Bannocks reached the village, Hawk and Jim still observing them from a distance, the uproar that accompanied their successful hunt was immediately muted. Hawk could hear the sudden shrieking lamentations at the sight of Little Swagger's dead body. The tribe's grief was genuine and terrible, born of the knowledge that with Little Swagger's death, his woman and offspring and all his relatives were left without a warrior or a hunter to see them through all the winters yet to come.

Hearing the cries and lamentations, Hawk steeled himself and did not let it affect him. Little Swagger would never have felt Hawk's cold blade had he not joined in the killing of Singing Wind. Peering out through the pines with Jim, Hawk waited, unmoved, for the reaction his calculated use of the lance was bound to elicit. It was not long in coming. A day later Scalped, Big Jaw, and Red Paint rode out of the camp astride their finest war ponies.

They knew Hawk was nearby, waiting, and they had accepted his challenge.

*   *   *

For the next two days Hawk and Jim, astride their mounts, led the three Bannocks through rough country, careful to remain just out of reach. On the second day, as they had planned, the two riders split, one heading west, the other south. Their tracks in the broad, snow-blanketed valley were easy enough to follow. The only question in Hawk's mind was which of the three Bannocks would follow him, and which Jim. As dusk fell that night, Hawk realized his pursuer was the Bannock he called Scalped.

Hawk could not have been more pleased. He camped beneath a rock shelf, digging out the snow until he came upon dry tinder. Then he gathered some reasonably dry pine branches and built a roaring fire. Fashioning a rough spit, he roasted a snowshoe rabbit he had shot the day before. He had just about finished the rabbit when he saw Scalped coming up the steep slope toward him.

Hawk was not surprised. His fire had been an open invitation to the Bannock, and Scalped was accepting it.

It was completely dark by this time. The snow was deep and Scalped had a difficult time leading his horse through it. Hawk was in no particular danger. With the great, towering rock wall at his back, this frontal route was the only one open to the Bannock.

Hawk finished eating the rabbit and tossed the bones to one side. Then he wiped his greasy fingers on the thighs of his buckskin and picked up his rifle—it was already loaded and primed—and watched Scalped leave his horse behind as he continued on up the steep slope, his grim, painted face reflecting the light from Hawk's fire.

When he caught sight of Hawk braced against the rock wall beside the campfire, the Indian pulled up without a word. He carried a lance and a bow, and there was a large skinning knife with a curved blade stuck in his breechclout's waistband. He had a quiver slung over his back. It was decorated with ermine fur. Folding his arms proudly, the Bannock stared up at Hawk. His partially scalped head looked ugly, and in order to cover the bald spot, the Indian combed his hair over it, fastening it with painted quills. Since the warrior had evidently made a deal with the Comanche who had come after him, Hawk decided to speak in the Comanche tongue.

"Before we do battle," he told the Bannock, "I would like to know one thing. How are you called?"

The reply was in passable Comanche. "Little Horse."

"How was the Comanche called?"

"Two Hatchet."

Hawk raised the rifle to his shoulder. "Thank you, Little Horse. Now I am going to kill you."

Little Horse laughed. "So this is how the terrible Golden Hawk does battle with his enemies? He dares not stand and fight like a true warrior. He uses his long rifle instead. So he is like any other white man. He does not live in the trees. He is not the Great Cannibal Owl. And now, afraid of combat, he will shoot Little Horse."

"It is the surest way I know of killing you," Hawk told him calmly, pulling back the hammer.

"That woman of yours, she was very good," cried the Bannock, "before we stripped the skin from her body. Do you not want to punish me for such a deed?"

Hawk lowered the rifle and eased the hammer forward.

Little Horse grinned when he saw Hawk lower the rifle. "Here I am," he said. "Come down here and punish me."

Hawk hesitated. He knew what the Bannock was up to, but he also knew how sweet it would be for him to feel Little Horse's neck beneath his fingers.

"Many times we took your woman," Little Horse taunted. "So many times that she forgot to struggle." He grinned up at Hawk. "I think she liked it. When we stopped, she begged for more. But we were tired of her. So then we peel her skin. She cried out then and begged for death, but we kept her alive for a long, long time. It was good to see the woman of Golden Hawk cry out like this."

Hawk took a step closer to the Bannock.

"It was too bad she died after only two days. We had much more we wanted to do to her. I gave her water at the end to keep her alive, but it did no good. So I piss on her."

With a cry that rent the night, Hawk flung himself at Little Horse. He was in midair when he struck him. Grappling wildly, the two tumbled and rolled back down the slope. When they halted finally in a ridged snowbank and sprang to their feet, Hawk's only weapon was his bowie and all Little Horse held was his long, curved skinning knife. They drew momentarily apart, looking for an opening as their eyes adjusted to the bright, moonlit slope.

They feinted once or twice warily. But the footing in the deep snow was treacherous and neither could manage a strong enough lunge. The Bannock was facing up the slope. Hawk lowered his shoulder and slammed into the warrior's midsection, toppling him backward into the snowbank. Hawk came to rest on top of him. Little Horse's knife flashed up at him, like a gleaming tongue. Hawk rolled back and slashed at the Indian's wrist with his bowie. The powerful blade severed the Bannock's hand from his wrist. Hawk could see the blood gouting darkly from the Indian's stump.

Hawk jumped up and stepped back into the snow drift to wait. Little Horse was still game. With his left hand he groped in the snow for his knife, and when he found it, he started for Hawk on all fours. Hawk stepped back, measured carefully, and kicked the Indian in the face, flipping him over onto his back. Then he snatched away the Bannock's knife and flung it down the slope.

Straightening up, Hawk stared down at the

form twisting slowly in the dark, growing patch of slush. Little Horse would soon bleed to death, Hawk realized. Not a bad way to die. He would gradually get weaker, lose consciousness, and soon be dead. It would be like going to sleep, Hawk realized angrily, the Bannock's taunting words about Singing Wind still echoing in his head.

Turning, Hawk went back up the slope, found the bow and the lance, and returned to the Bannock.

Hawk peered down at the dying Indian. He was like Singing Wind must have been at the end. He could still feel pain, even though he was too weak to fight back. Hawk stood carefully over the Bannock and buried the head of his lance in the Indian's gut. Then, reaching past the Bannock's head, Hawk selected an arrow from his quiver and sent it into his chest.

For the first time the Bannock cried out. A grim, satisfied smile on his face, Hawk squatted beside the dying Bannock and finished scalping him.

— 7 —

Pushing his mount hard, Hawk came upon Jim's tracks and those of his two Bannock pursuers three days later. He was close to Grizzly Pass by this time and did not find the body of the first Bannock until late in the day. It was Big Jaw. He was sprawled on his back in the snow, a neat bullet hole drilled in his forehead.

The Bannock's horse trailed off from there, its tracks disappearing down the slope, while the tracks of the remaining Bannock continued on, heading for Grizzly Pass. Studying the sign, Hawk saw where the second Bannock, the one they had christened Red Paint, had jumped from his horse to examine his dead companion, then pulled his horse into a hollow before continuing on to the pass after Jim.

It was past dusk when Hawk held up inside

the pass and made camp on a slope high above the Indian's tracks. He awoke the next morning to find it was snowing steadily, the shifting curtain of gray-white enough to blot out completely the contours of the valley below him. After a meager meal of jerky and melted snow, he mounted up and continued on into the pass. A little before noon, he caught sight of a trampled, uneven patch of snow in the distance and turned his horse toward it.

Dismounting, he started for what looked the snow-covered torso of a dead Indian. It was curiously twisted and unnatural-looking. Hawk had almost reached it when his foot struck something round and unyielding through the snow. Hawk bent and picked it up. When he finished brushing off the snow, he found himself looking into the startled face of the beheaded Bannock, his red war paint smeared over his dead features. Hawk tossed the grisly head away and glanced over at the torso in the snow. He realized why it looked so strange: there was no head on its shoulders.

Hawk glanced down at the trampled snow. It was obvious the Indian had put up quite a fight before Jim finished him off. And the struggle had evidently occurred not too long ago—or all signs of it would have vanished by now under the steady snowfall. Hawk mounted up and continued on. In less than an hour he found himself overtaking a rider, seen only dimly through the snow that continued to sift down out of the gray skies. Hawk was pretty sure it was Jim, but he could not be positive. As he increased his horse's pace, the rider ahead of him slipped from his horse, allowing his mount to continue on. Regaining his footing almost immediately, the rider attempted to overtake his horse. But in a matter of seconds, as silent as a ghost, the horse vanished ahead of him into the snow.

By that time Hawk knew for sure he had found Jim Clyman, the mountain man's great rawboned height and massive shoulders allowing no room for doubt. Hawk cupped his hands about his mouth and called out to him.

Jim halted in the waist-deep snow and turned.

Hawk rode on a ways farther, then dismounted and plowed toward Jim through the deep snow, pulling his horse behind him. Before Hawk reached him, the mountain man sank into the snow, exhausted.

"You took your time, Hawk."

"Came as soon as I could. But hell, Jim, from the look of it, you didn't need me."

He grinned crookedly. "Guess not."

Hawk leaned close to his friend. One glimpse of the fearful rent in Jim Clyman's buckskin shirt and the bloody bandage Jim had managed to wrap around his chest told Hawk Jim's wound was a serious one.

"How'd it happen?" Hawk asked.

"Got careless with Red Paint. Thought I'd killed him with one shot. Always a stupid assumption, that. When I rolled him over, he came alive good and proper. We went at each other with knives. His caught me in the chest before I was able to take off his head with mine."

"I came across it in the snow."

"I got lucky. He had his knife in me, but I took a wild swipe with my knife and caught him just right."

"He'll have a hell of a time hunting in the next world without a head."

Jim grinned. "I thought of that."

Dimly through the snow Hawk saw a patch of timber off to his left. He helped Jim onto his own horse, then led Jim into the timber, where he found some shelter under a dense tangle of berry vines and mountain laurel over which the snow had formed a roof. The place gave them protection from the wind and made a decent-enough camp, as the snow showed no sign of letting up. A fire was out of the question, so Hawk contented himself with making Jim as comfortable as possible, wrapping him in both Jim's slicker and his own.

He decided against searching for Jim's horse. Darkness was falling swiftly and there was always the chance he would get lost. In what little light remained, he examined the knife wound in Jim's chest. It looked ugly enough, and from the size of the hole it was obvious Jim must have lost considerable blood. Outside of that, Hawk could tell very little. He would know more if the wound began to smell or if Jim started coughing up blood. So far, Jim did not have a fever. He was pretty weak, but considering how much blood Jim must have lost, that was perfectly natural.

Jim dined greedily on what remained of Hawk's jerky, then slept. Hawk slept also and awoke the next morning to a cold, silent world. The snow had stopped, but the temperature must have dropped to well below zero—maybe ten or even twenty degrees—and it felt like it was still going down. Hawk found he had to push up against the tangle of vines and branches resting on his shoulder. The thick blanket of snow had pressed it down considerably. Beside him, Jim pushed himself upright also. His face looked flushed and his eyes overly bright.

"Hungry?" Hawk asked.

"I am that."

"How do you feel?"

"Stiff, and I got a mean headache."

Hawk was not surprised. Jim had a fever. Hawk was by now keenly aware of his own empty stomach. Fresh game was needed if either of them were to survive long enough to return to the fort. He crawled out from under the shelter and found a spot out in the open for a campfire, then spent a considerable time scraping away the snow and gathering tinder and pine branches for a fire. Once he had produced a good blaze with enough firewood to keep it going, he loaded his Hawken. He was careful not to touch the metal with his bare hands. It was that cold. During the previous winter, high in Shoshone country, Hawk had experienced cold so intense it had split trees open with a crack resembling gunfire. But this late in the winter it was not likely to get that cold, he hoped.

"I won't be long," Hawk told Jim as he started out.

"You won't be taking the horse?"

"It's too weak."

"Good luck."

"I'll need it."

But by midday the only luck he had was bad. Outside of some wolves on a ridge high above the pass, the only live animal he had seen was a single hawk. Later he caught sight of a duck, but no sign of grouse or sage hen and no sign of deer or elk. On the mountain slopes above him he could see no snow paths. In his eagerness to bag some fresh meat, Hawk kept going longer than he should have. He realized his mistake when dusk overtook him on his way back to camp with a mile or so still to go before he would reach it.

Since late afternoon the wolf pack he had seen on the ridge above the pass had descended to the plain and were keeping pace with him. They were probably as famished as Hawk was. The darker it became, the closer to Hawk they drifted. Hawk was slightly nervous, recalling the pack that had raided the settlers—until something occurred to him, and he smiled suddenly. Why,

here, just out of reach of his rifle, was the
very meat he had been seeking all day. Though
wolf meat was not much higher on the scale than
dog meat, right now that made precious little
difference.

Checking his load, Hawk pulled up to wait for
the wolves to get closer. Not counting the leader,
there were five wolves in all, strung out well
behind the big fellow. There was a good chance,
Hawk realized, that these wolves were a rem-
nant of the pack that had attacked the settlers
earlier. That had sure as hell been a bold and
murderous bunch. Yet the wolves' respect for
Hawk was such that as soon as Hawk halted,
they pulled up also and sank watchfully into the
snow. Only the pack's leader seemed willing to
get much closer than his fellows.

Hawk waited, but the leader was too smart for
him and began circling Hawk just out of range.
By this time the other wolves were almost out of
sight in the snow. But they were there, Hawk
knew, watching ... and waiting. It was said
wolves knew when a man carried a gun.

The pack leader was a big fellow. Hawk judged
him to weigh at least 140 pounds or more. As he
continued to move slowly around him, Hawk could
see his tongue lolling between his lower canines,
his ears forward, his mouth open. It looked as if
he were wondering what Hawk was doing in
wolf country this late in the day.

Hawk cursed silently. Here was his meat. Wolf

meat. Just out of reach of his Hawken. All he had to do was lure the big wolf closer. But that seemed impossible. Wolves weren't dumb, and the sight of Hawk's rifle was keeping the big wolf—and the rest of his pack—well back and out of harm's way.

What the wolves were waiting for, Hawk realized, was for him to make camp and fall asleep. Many a mountain man had found that with a fire down and a man asleep in his blanket, a wolf pack, driven by hunger, would attack. All it took was for the wolves to be certain they had a victim, one who could not fight back, like a wounded doe, or an elk caught on the ice, or a snowshoe rabbit nailed against a tree.

Or a man down.

Hawk frowned and thought that over. Earlier, with the pack keeping pace with him, he had told himself not to fall down or appear to be weak or floundering in the heavy snow.

Now he decided that had been exactly the wrong advice. He started up briskly enough. There was still light left in the sky, and the unbroken tablecloth of unblemished snow stretching out before him gave the pass a pale, unearthly glow. The cold was terrible, but there was no wind. Only when he started up again and felt how stiff his toes and joints were did Hawk realize how dangerously cold it had become.

The pack kept pace with him, as Hawk had known it would. After a quarter of a mile, Hawk

stumbled and sprawled forward into the snow.
He waited a considerable time, then pushed himself upright. The pack had closed around him,
but at the sight of him heaving himself upright,
they turned and swiftly distanced themselves.
Hawk did not even bother to lift his rifle to his
shoulder.

But he was sure now he would have wolf meat
for that night's meal.

He started up again, trudging along, pumping
the blood through his veins. When he had reached
a point where a rest in the snow would not chill
him dangerously, he again stumbled and sprawled
forward, letting his rifle slip from his hands. He
got up after a while, staggered forward a few
more paces, then collapsed again. After a short
while he began to struggle on his hands and
knees through the snow, until at last he sprawled
forward, then rolled over onto his back and lay
still, perfectly still. His bowie knife clutched in
his right hand, he waited, looking up at the world
from under his nearly closed eyelids. After a
while he saw the bright moon rise up and sit on a
distant, pine-covered ridge.

The cold was beginning to seep into his bones
and he wished the wolves would hurry—their
leader, anyway. He was beginning to think he
had misjudged him—that the big gaunt leader of
the pack did not have the courage needed to
attack a man in the open like this—when he
found himself staring into the wolf's eyes.

This close, the wolf was much bigger than Hawk had guessed. He had come up so quietly that he seemed almost to have materialized in front of him. The wolf did not look at Hawk's right hand. His eyes met Hawk's and did not flinch away. The fellow's big tongue was still lolling between his clean white canines, steam billowing up from his open mouth. The eyes had large round black holes for pupils and irises that looked pale green in the moonlight. The wolf's face did not seem ferocious—only curious. But Hawk knew the long gaunt body was trembling from hunger.

But Hawk was no less hungry than this wolf.

Growling, the wolf lowered his head, fastening his eyes on Hawk's neck. Hawk felt the hair on the back of his neck rising. At the same time he remembered his battle with an earlier wolf—one just as determined. The wolf stopped growling. His eyes went opaque. Just in time Hawk flung up his left forearm and felt the wolf's jaw clamp down, his teeth unable to bite clean through Hawk's wolfskin sleeve. Rolling swiftly over onto the wolf, Hawk pinned the animal under him and plunged his knife repeatedly into his exposed chest. As the wolf cried out in shocked yelps, Hawk heard a snarling bark and turned to face two other wolves charging across the snowfield toward him.

Hawk jumped up and ran back for his rifle. He knew the firing caps were drenched and made no effort to fire as the closest wolf leapt at him. He swung the rifle barrel and caught the animal flush on the side of the head. As the wolf went tumbling into a snowbank, its companion veered quickly away and ran back to join its friends.

Breathing heavily, sweat freezing on his forehead, Hawk walked over to the second wolf. The Hawken's rifle barrel had smashed through its skull and the wolf lay on its back in the snow, stretched out to its full length, no longer breathing. Hawk went back to the pack leader. He was dead. Fine.

Wasting no time, Hawk slung both dead animals over his shoulders and proceeded on through the moonlit night to his camp in the timber. Twice during the long trek, the enormous weight of the two dead animals forced him to sink into the snow to regain his wind. Each time he looked back to see if what remained of the wolf pack was still following him. But the wolves had vanished.

Now maybe they would spread the word to any other wolves in the neighborhood. A man with a knife can be just as dangerous as one with a rifle.

Hawk found Jim unconscious, the fire nearly out. He rapidly built up the fire, melted some snow, and made coffee. It was the aroma of the coffee that revived Jim, and when Hawk then set to dressing the two wolves, Jim grew even more alert. Later, sitting up with one of the wolf's roasted haunches in his hand, Jim was ready to admit he might live.

"I tell you, Hawk," he said hoarsely, "I'm through with this high country."

"Where you going, then?"

"Californy, that's where." His teeth tore off a chunk of steaming flesh. "Why, hoss, it's always summer there. And they have the prettiest little Spanish ladies you ever did see livin' there. Pretty and happy and they don't wear no petticoats, neither."

"Makes it easy, does it?"

"You bet it does!"

"What'll you do there? Trap?"

"Sure. And raise horses. They got more horses in Californy than we got buffalo here. It's a rich land, hoss. You ought to come, too."

"I got business this side of the mountains."

"With that Comanche?"

"And my sister. She's in these mountains somewhere."

"I hope you find her, Hawk. And then maybe you'll come visit me in a land where the sun shines all the time. You might say men like us deserve it, since there's a good chance when we die, we won't have it so good."

"Hell, Jim, it'll be pretty warm down there, too—or so I hear."

Jim laughed. Only he shouldn't have. The laughing led to coughing—uncontrolled coughing. Jim dropped the haunch he had been devouring so hungrily and doubled over, still coughing. Hawk didn't know what to do, so he did nothing—even when blood began pouring out of Jim's mouth.

After a long while, Jim stopped coughing. He mopped his mouth and chin with his sleeve and grinned feebly over at Hawk. "Guess maybe wolf meat don't agree with me."

"It wasn't the wolf meat."

Jim nodded bleakly. "You're right. I just et too much. Made a pig of myself."

"Just take it slow and easy, Jim."

"I'll do that," Jim said weakly, reaching for the haunch he had dropped.

But Jim only took a few more bites, chewed halfheartedly, then without a word crawled into their shelter, curled up in his blanket, and closed his eyes. He was obviously in great pain. His breath came in painful wheezes. He did not sound good and he did not look good.

Hawk finished his own haunch, flung the bone into the night, then got up and wedged the rest of the dressed wolf meat between two branches of the nearest pine tree, making sure it was high enough to keep it out of the reach of any desperate coyotes. By the time this chore was completed, Jim was asleep on his back, snoring with his mouth open, dead to the world. The heavy meal had knocked him out.

Working swiftly, Hawk leaned into the shelter, ripped off the bandage Jim had wrapped around his chest, and held a lighted piece of firewood over the wound. One of Jim's ribs had been broken; its jagged edge was ripping into Jim's left lung. With such a wound Jim could not possibly last the journey back to Fort Hall, Hawk realized, no matter how many wolves Hawk killed for him.

With a grim, fatalistic shrug, Hawk held the torch with his left hand and poked his bowie into the wound with his other. The tip of the knife caught the edge of the cracked rib. Hawk pulled up and was lucky enough to straighten out the rib. Fresh blood bubbled up from the rent in the lung and Jim came awake on the instant, a cry frozen on his lips.

"My God," he gasped. "What did you do, Hawk?"

"Straightened out your rib," Hawk said, pulling back from Jim. "It was cutting into your lung."

"Feels like hell!"

"Sorry."

"But it feels better than it did."

"Then go back to sleep."

"You goin' to do any more operatin'?"

"No."

"If you do, wait'll I get back to sleep."

The next day Jim seemed a little better, but Hawk waited until Jim's fever abated and the wound in his chest closed up before starting back to Fort Hall. The cold snap had intensified, and Jim suffered the worst from it as he was forced to ride Hawk's horse due to his weakened condition. Hawk, leading the horse and breaking ground for him through the deep snow, was grateful for the exertion. It kept him warm and his limbs free of frostbite.

A week later, when the last of the wolf meat was gone, Hawk's rifle brought down a big elk buck. Not long afterward, when the two men reached Fort Hall, they were able to share the kill with Mac Gregor and the rest of the fort's inhabitants—all of whom, it seemed, were ravenous for fresh meat.

Alice and two other settlers' wives attended to Jim Clyman as he was brought into Mac Gregor's quarters for treatment. At first it was thought he must lose his toes to frostbite, but Jim insisted they would be all right and refused the traditional remedy for frostbite: a good scrubbing with handfuls of fresh snow. Instead, he insisted that warm blankets be wrapped around his feet and hands. And once this was done, he told the women to leave him be so he could sleep.

Hawk laughed at Jim's curt dismissal of the three women and turned to them apologetically. "Jim's a very tired man," he explained. "Let him get some sleep now. Thank you for coming."

Mac Gregor had been standing to one side. He moved quickly back to the door and opened it. With a gallant bow, he ushered the three women out of his room. Alice Gentry was the last to leave. As she stepped through the doorway, she looked back at Hawk.

"You must be tired also, Hawk," she reminded him. Then she smiled. "My door is always open."

"Thank you, Alice," he said.

The door closed behind her and Hawk turned back to Jim.

"You better get after that one," Jim told Hawk. "She's too nice to pass up."

"Never mind that. How do you feel?"

"I'll be tramping all over Californy, come spring."

Hawk grinned. "I sure hope so."

"You can bet on it."

"I will."

Then Hawk bid Jim good night, nodded to Mac Gregor, and left the room.

Alice Gentry's eyes gleamed with pleasure as she opened her door to him. Reaching out, she took both of his hands in hers and drew him gratefully into her arms. Hawk kicked the door shut, lifted her in his arms, and carried her into the bedroom. It was warm in Alice Gentry's apartment, the bed was soft, as were her breasts and lips, and he did not ever again want to be as cold as he had been these past weeks.

"Mmm," Alice said as she swiftly unbuttoned her blouse. He was already peeling his buckskins past his hips. "You can have these breasts to play with for a while; then I am going to prepare a bath for you."

"Will you join me in the tub?"

"Can we fit?"

"We'll fit, all right."

She laughed. "Yes," she said. "I guess we will."

After the bath and what followed, Hawk lay in

Alice Gentry's arms and brushed his hand playfully over her nipples. He was not through yet, and he was beginning to wonder if he would ever be able to get enough of Alice Gentry. She laughed softly, leaned closer, and nibbled playfully on one of his earlobes.

"Must you go so soon, Hawk?" she whispered.

"It can't be helped."

She rested her cheek on his broad chest and snaked her arms around him, hugging him gently. "At least wait until the winter breaks."

"What makes you think it will?"

She laughed. "It has to. It's almost March."

"I want to get this business with Two Hatchet over with."

He had not told Alice about Singing Wind. This was a secret wound, and the pain of his loss was not something he felt the need to share with others. All he had told Alice was that Two Hatchet was a Comanche who had come north seeking him, and that Hawk felt an obligation to return the favor. And that meant a trip south to the Staked Plains of Texas.

"When you come back from Texas," she reminded him softly, "I might be gone."

"That's a chance I'll have to take, Alice."

"No, it isn't."

"What do you mean?"

"If you say so, I'll stay here and wait for you. When you return, we could travel to California together—without all that nonsense of a wagon train."

Frowning, Hawk gave the suggestion serious thought. "We could, at that," he muttered.

Alice lifted her head off his chest and stared eagerly down at him. "You mean you might?"

He grinned up at her. "Might what?"

"You heard me. Go with me to California, if I wait here for you."

"How do you know I'll make it back? Two Hatchet might kill me. Or any other member of the band."

"Then why go all the way down there in the first place?"

"I told you. I want to end this foolishness."

She dropped her head back onto his chest. "Don't you know?" she said gloomily. "That kind of foolishness goes on forever. Stay here until spring, then go with me to California. Forget that crazy Comanche tribe. You're not a part of them now. That's all behind you."

He stroked her hair. Perhaps he should do as she suggested. Maybe he could forget Two Hatchet and the part he had played in Singing Wind's death. And maybe someday he would forget Singing Wind as well.

But how could he ever forget his sister, Annabelle?

He cupped Alice's face in his big hands and lifted her head gently off his chest, then rolled easily over onto her. She smiled up at him in anticipation and, like a big cat stretching, opened her thighs. He moved up easily until he was deep inside her lovely warmth. He bent and kissed her on the lips. She answered his kiss and tightened both arms around his neck.

Then she started to say something.

"Shh," he told her softly. "No more talk."

She nodded and began to thrust her pelvis gently. They rocked softly together, as close as two people ever get, and talked no more about California or Two Hatchet that night.

— 8 —

He had almost left winter behind. But there was still a chill wind at his back as he pulled his horse to a halt and gazed down the long valley at the Arapaho winter encampment set in among the giant cottonwoods that lined the stream. The surrounding prairie grass had not yet recovered from the winter's blasts, and patches of snow dotted its rolling surface, but the promise of spring was in the air on the heels of a wind that was no longer biting.

Still in Arapaho country, Hawk had not yet reached the Arkansas River. He had made the decision earlier to confront the Arapaho directly in order to gain safe passage through their country. And since he would make it clear he was intent on punishing Comanches, there was a chance the Arapaho might offer to escort him part of the way.

Hawk nudged his horse down the slope, splashed across the icy stream, and then rode close along the riverbank until he was within hailing distance of the village. By that time he had been discovered and warriors from the village came trotting up on horses, the women and children and old ones tagging along behind them.

Hawk held up his hand, palm out, in the traditional sign of friendship that all Plains Indians honored. The greeting was returned by a young Arapaho chief who cantered out to greet him. He was a handsome man with a strong blade of a nose; he wore a necklace of grizzly-bear claws. Hawk continued on until he reached the chief and pulled up as the rest of the warriors fanned out around him. In a moment Hawk found himself ringed by a solid rank of inscrutable, curious faces. Like any good Plains Indian, Hawk sat well back on his horse on a saddle stripped to its barest essentials; yet he wore the buckskins of a white trader and his eyes were blue, his long hair blond.

Aware that this close to Comanche country many of the Arapaho knew the tongue of their traditional enemies, Hawk spoke to the Arapaho chief facing him in the Comanche tongue.

"I come in peace," he said, "and seek the famed hospitality of the mighty Arapaho."

The chief glanced at another Arapaho, who nudged his horse alongside the chief's. This Arapaho was older than the chief and considerably battle-scarred. His upper lip was sliced off and from it a scar ran under his chin. His dark eyes regarded Hawk malevolently.

"How does white man speak Comanche?" this one asked Hawk in passable Comanche.

"For many years I was Comanche slave."

At once the malevolence in the scarred Indian's eyes changed to recognition, then wonder. He spoke rapidly to the chief, who immediately became as excited as he.

The scarred Indian turned his attention back to Hawk. "We of the Arapaho Nation know of you. You are Golden Hawk."

Hawk was not really surprised they had heard of him. It was getting almost impossible for him to outrun his notoriety. "Yes," he admitted calmly, "I am Golden Hawk."

The chief nodded approvingly to the scarred one, who turned eagerly back to Hawk. "I am Scar. This is Bear Claw, war chief of the Arapaho. He would be honored to share his lodge with the great killer of Comanches. Come now and join us in celebration of your famous exploits."

With a nod Hawk thanked the chief. Like wind across prairie grass, word of Hawk's identity had long since spread to these mounted warriors around him and to the rest of the tribe as well. The mounted Indians closed about Hawk, and with the chief and Scar in the lead, Hawk was escorted proudly into the village, the women and children and the older people running alongside him. With graphic motions of their arms and with high-pitched yells they showed Hawk how eager they were to welcome the already legendary killer of Comanches.

All this was considerably more than Hawk had bargained for when he decided to approach the Arapaho village, yet he realized he could not possibly insult the Arapaho by refusing join in their welcoming festivities. It had been a long winter; spring was at hand. A celebration was in order, and Hawk's arrival had become the perfect excuse for one.

Long past midnight—his head reeling from the food and drink, the noise and the smoke and the dancing—Hawk found himself in the chief's lodge wrestling with a dark-eyed hellion who was determined to have Golden Hawk sink his shaft deep within her before morning broke over the village. Despite his state of exhaustion bordering on drunkenness, she had managed to arouse him enough to enable her to engulf his feeble erection within her warm moistness when another dark-haired Arapaho maiden joined the first and insisted on sharing Hawk.

On his back Hawk looked up groggily at the first Arapaho woman sitting astride him and saw her flailing away at the second. The violent activity between the two women was beginning to have its effect on him, and just as he started to take eager wing under the first, Bear Claw entered the tepee, saw the difficulty, grabbed the second woman by the hair, and flung her out through the entrance.

With a high, keening cry of delight, the first one turned her complete attention back to Hawk, leaned her hands on his shoulders, and began pumping furiously, sweat rolling down her naked torso. In the dim light from the single candle, Hawk looked past her and saw the light in Bear Claw's eyes as he watched. He hustled over to his own woman sleeping on the far side of the tepee and nudged her twice, anxiously. But she pretended to be asleep.

At once Bear Claw disappeared back out through the entrance, to return a moment later with the young woman he had just evicted. He flung her down on his mat and joined Hawk in the festivities. Hawk paid little attention as he hung on for as long as he could, then let go while his woman pounded him happily on his chest and continued to rock feverishly as she built to her own climax. He remembered her body slapping hard down upon his, her chin digging into his shoulder.

Then came blessed sleep.

When Hawk awoke the next morning, the villagers were already celebrating the imminent departure of their warriors. Drums were beating and old men were singing their war songs, while the women were already decorating the manes and tails of their husbands' war ponies with flowers and ribbons. Blinking in the sunlight, Hawk stood in front of Bear Claw's lodge, observing all the activity. The third dish of dog meat since he had arrived in this village sat heavily in his stomach. He belched unhappily and realized what he had not fully grasped during the previous night's hectic celebration. With Hawk's magic on their side, Chief Scar had decided that now would be the perfect time for Arapaho warriors to raid the Kwahadi Comanche and take at least one of their fine herds of war ponies.

Hawk understood the chief's reasoning. With the magic of Golden Hawk on their side, how could they fail? According to the gossip that reached every council fire on the plains, Hawk had already killed every Kwahadi that had gone after him. If Golden Hawk was not really capable of transforming himself into the Great Cannibal Owl, as some whispered, he was certainly a warrior who had proven he was more than a match for any Comanche.

But as Hawk rode out that afternoon at the head of close to thirty Arapaho warriors, the eager Chief Scar riding at his side as the war party's leader, he found himself more than a little disturbed by this development. He had no desire to lead this large war party against the people he had lived with for so long—even if during that time he had been little more than the Comanche's slave. Though he wanted Two Hatchet's death and had every intention of returning the Comanche warrior's lance to him personally, as he had told Alice Gentry, what he really wanted was an end to the People sending braves after him. If he could speak to old Buffalo Hump, chief of the Comanche band that had captured him, Hawk was certain he could work out some kind of truce with the band.

But certainly there would be no truce if he led an Arapaho raid on their village.

A day later they crossed the Arkansas River into Comanche territory. The Staked Plains were still a three-day ride farther southwest—time enough, Hawk hoped, for him to figure a way out of his dilemma. But when they at last made camp a short distance from the Comanche village, all Hawk had come up with was an open and unequivocal betrayal of the Arapaho, something he was loathe to do. They had greeted him with such warmth and seemed so pleased to be riding at his side.

But Hawk had no choice. At the first opportunity he would break away from the Arapaho war party and warn the village.

It was dawn and the sky to the east was already alight with the first faint glow of day. Hawk was pleased, certain his flight from the Arapaho camp had been accomplished without detection. Then he heard the hard pounding of unshod hooves behind him and turned his horse in time to meet Scar's headlong rush. Hurling himself from the back of his pony, the chief grabbed Hawk about his waist and dragged him off his horse. Hawk came down hard on his back, the infuriated Arapaho on top of him.

"You are traitor to the Arapaho," he accused in Comanche. "You go to warn your Comanche brothers."

As Scar spoke, he closed his fingers about

Hawk's throat. Hawk flung himself backward and twisted, breaking the Arapaho's grip. Then he jumped up and moved back and away from Scar's hatchet, its steel blade glinting in the early morning light. Scar lunged as Hawk ducked aside, trying to think of something to say to placate the enraged chief.

But before he could, Scar flung his hatchet, then charged. Hawk ducked low as the hatchet flew past, then he held his ground and punched the Indian flush on the side of his jaw. It was a wicked blow that snapped Scar's head completely around, stopping him in his tracks. But he shook off the blow's effects with a single snap of his head, lowered it, came on once again. Twice more Hawk pounded the chief about his head and shoulders, but it seemed to have no effect on him. With a roar like that of an enraged bear, Scar flung his arms about Hawk's waist, grappling with incredible strength as he fell forward onto Hawk.

Hawk had not wanted to wound Scar. But he saw now that he had no choice. Gasping, he managed to draw his bowie. With a deep grunt of annoyance, Scar slapped away the knife and released Hawk. Darting past Hawk, he snatched up his hatchet and brought it down. Hawk just managed to duck out of the way. Before Scar could come at him again with the hatchet, Hawk kicked him in the face, snapping his head back violently. Scar dropped the hatchet and slammed down onto his back, blinking dazedly up at Hawk.

Snatching up the hatchet, Hawk leapt astride him and brought the hatchet's handle down upon Scar's Adam's apple, applying considerable pressure.

Scar fought with silent tenacity, trying desperately to dislodge Hawk. But Hawk only increased the pressure on the warrior's throat until the chief lay still, eyes wide, trying desperately to breathe.

"Listen to me, Chief," Hawk told him in harsh Comanche. "The Golden Hawk did not ask for you or the other Arapaho warriors to join him. He does not need their help and he does not want it. Take your warriors back to their village and think no more of taking Comanche ponies."

Then, carefully, Hawk eased back on the hatchet's handle to get Scar's response.

Scar was still defiant. Gasping painfully, he glared up at Hawk. "You are not more than any other man," he rasped, his voice barely audible. "You have no medicine to help the Arapaho."

Hawk smiled and nodded. "That is so, Chief."

"You are like all white men. You lie!"

"You did not hear me lie, Chief. How can I help what wild tales are told around the fire by old men and women? Do not listen to these tales, Chief. I am only a man like any other."

"And so is each Comanche a man like any other. Go! Warn them! It will make no difference. Soon, Arapaho warriors will sweep through their village and take as many scalps and ponies as they wish. Now kill me. Do it. I am not afraid to die!"

Hawk leaned forward once again and felt the handle bearing down on the chief's Adam's apple. If Hawk did not ease up, he knew, the chief's windpipe would shatter. Hawk could not do it. He felt no hatred for Scar. Pulling back suddenly, Hawk struck the chief on the side of his head with the face of the hatchet's blade. The blow broke no bones and drew no blood, but it was enough to render the Arapaho warrior senseless, and that was sufficient for Hawk's purposes.

Retrieving his knife, Hawk swung into his saddle. He looked down and saw that Scar, though still unconscious, was breathing normally and would recover his senses soon enough. Hawk had no doubt that when he did, he would waste no time leading his warriors in an attack—whether the Comanches were forewarned or not. Scar was a brave, stubborn warrior.

And a foolish one as well.

— 9 —

Glancing back in the direction of the Arapaho encampment, Hawk saw the horizon come alive with Arapaho horsemen. They were closing in fast and he could barely hear their war cries. Something was up, and they knew it. When they found their chief, they would know for sure what it was.

He turned his mount and lashed it to a sudden gallop, soon reaching the outskirts of the Kwahadi village. It was full daylight now, and the dogs met him first, running at his horse and nipping at its heels. The children came next. Charging into the village past them and ignoring the warriors who came hurrying from their lodges to catch a glimpse of him, Hawk pulled his horse to a halt in front of the lodge of an old chief, recognizing the design on its sides. Hawk slipped

Comanche-fashion from his horse and strode over to the entrance just as Hank-of-Hair, Buffalo Hump's wife, peered out at him, then stuck her head back inside.

Hawk came to a stop at once and waited—not too patiently. In his hand he held the lance belonging to Two Hatchet.

Buffalo Hump, stooping only slightly, stepped out through the entrance, then straightened and gazed at Hawk. His face slightly more wrinkled and his hair thinner and a shade whiter, it seemed the old chief had changed little in the years since Hawk broke free of the band. Buffalo Hump was as impassive and as inscrutable as ever. Only his large, opaque black eyes gave any indication of the amazement he felt at Hawk's return.

Behind him Hank-of-Hair peered out of the tepee, her wrinkled face revealing none of the contempt and fury Hawk knew she felt for this hateful prodigal son whose return now could only mean trouble.

"I have come to warn you, Buffalo Hump."

"I am listening."

"Arapaho. They will be here soon. They have come to raid and take as many ponies as they can."

For a long moment the old chief regarded Hawk without responding. It was clear he was having great difficulty believing the words of one who had deceived him so often in the past. After all, was it not Hawk who had left his war party deep in Mexico, the blood of a famed war chief and who knew how many other brave Comanche warriors on his hands?

Now Buffalo Hump was being asked to believe that this scourge of his people—one whose exploits were sung with glee in every Plains Indian camp except Comanche—had returned to save them, to warn of an impending attack from an Arapaho enemy who had never dared enter Comanche territory in the memory of any Comanche there.

It was not easy to believe such a thing.

His shrewd eyes narrowing, Buffalo Hump said, "And how do you know this? Was it you brought them?"

"Never mind that. I tell you they are even now on their way. Hurry!"

"And will the Golden Hawk lead his brother Comanche against these foolish Arapaho?"

"I will. But you must arouse the camp. They will be here soon."

"This is another of your tricks, Scowls-at-the-People," Buffalo Hump said, addressing Hawk as the band used to address him. "But this time this old chief will not listen to your crooked tongue."

A young Mexican boy came running. As he ran, he shouted in Comanche and pointed at the hills beyond the village, the young herd-tender's words confirming Hawk's warning: a hard-charging line of Arapaho warriors had encircled the horse herds and had already cut out a large number. Other Arapaho warriors were cutting toward the village from downstream.

Hawk turned to Buffalo Hump. "Believe me now, Buffalo Hump. Save your people!"

Buffalo Hump gave the alarm. Hawk remounted and pulled his horse around to meet the Arapaho coming upstream. As he lifted his horse to a full gallop, he found six, then seven Comanche warriors joining him, and before he had reached the end of the village, he was leading a party of eleven Comanche. Looking back, he saw Buffalo Hump and at least half a dozen warriors galloping out to intercept the Arapaho encircling the horse herd.

Turning back around, Hawk wondered which of the Comanche horsemen riding with him or with Buffalo Hump was the warrior who called himself Two Hatchet.

Hawk caught sight of a very healthy Chief Scar leading at least twenty Arapaho warriors along the riverbank toward him. Letting loose with an earsplitting Comanche yell, Hawk urged his horse still faster as he led his outnumbered contingent directly toward the Arapaho war party. For a moment Chief Scar and the other Arapaho warriors pressed on. After all, they had an overwhelming advantage in numbers. But the sight of Golden Hawk and his onrushing Comanche force was too demoralizing. At the last possible moment the Arapaho broke ranks and veered away, heading in full flight for a distant ridge.

The shrill Comanche war cry broke from the warriors behind Hawk as they joined him in chasing the fleeing Arapaho. Just before the fleeing warriors reached the ridge, Hawk's smaller force overtook them. The heavy whisper of arrows filled the air. Rifles cracked, then were silent. There was no time for reloading. Hatchets, war clubs, and knives were brought into play as warrior met warrior in close hand-to-hand combat. Warriors tumbled or were dragged from their ponies as horses and men swirled about one another in one wild, shouting melee.

Hawk felt a hatchet strike his shoulder a glancing blow. He turned in time to be dragged from his horse by an Arapaho who had no time to repent his recklessness. Twisting himself in midair, Hawk kicked the Arapaho's legs out from under him, then fell upon him. With one vicious downward thrust of his bowie, he buried its blade deep in the warrior's chest. He pulled it free and looked up to see an Arapaho horseman pounding toward him.

Waiting until the last moment, Hawk ducked aside, then reached up and grabbed the Arapaho's thigh and flung him from his pony. The Arapaho's head struck the solid ground hard and broke under the impact like a rotted squash. Abruptly, just in front of Hawk, an Arapaho horse and rider went down under a storm of Comanche arrows. As the warrior struggled to pull himself from under his horse, Hawk finished his labors for him with a deep knife thrust to the jugular.

Abruptly the battlefield was silent, except for

the hoofbeats of two escaping Arapaho—one of them Chief Scar. Watching them vanish beyond the ridge, Hawk thought of going after them, but he was exhausted, as were those Comanche warriors who were still alive. Dazed but exuberant, they looked around at one another, hardly able to believe their good fortune. They had met a force almost twice their size and had routed it completely.

Leaving the scalping and mutilating of the hated Arapaho to the victorious Comanche, Hawk found his horse, mounted up, and rode back to the village, a hero once again to his former people.

The victory celebation ended a day later, and Hawk, on the invitation of Buffalo Hump, visited the old chief's lodge. As soon as he entered, Hank-of-Hair, her eyes glinting with hatred and mistrust, scurried from the tepee, saving one last, baleful glance for Hawk. Buffalo Hump took no notice of this. At this stage he was beyond doing anything to control his woman. So he pretended her exit had not taken place in the manner it had and motioned Hawk to a seat on a small pine-bough cushion across from his couch. Between them the hearth fire glowed, keeping the lodge warm. The nearly balmy weather of the past few days had given way once more to the icy blasts that swept down periodically from the north.

Buffalo Hump had already lit his pipe and sat puffing on it for some time before stirring himself and handing it across the hearth fire to Hawk, a rare honor that Hawk accepted gravely. Only when Hawk decided it was time to speak, did he hand the pipe back to Buffalo Hump. When he spoke, he was careful to observe the custom of not using a person's name in his presence.

"The wise and aged chief has been kind to allow this poor warrior to enter his lodge," Hawk said. "This white man—once a slave in his village—is grateful."

"The white warrior with gold hair has returned at last. Again he has shown with what courage and skill he strikes down the enemy. But he did not come back to save the People from the hateful Arapaho."

"That is true."

"The warrior has come back for Two Hatchet."

"Yes."

"The white warrior with the gold hair will soon look upon this Comanche. He has been sent for."

"This white man wishes to return the Comanche warrior's lance to him. Two Hatchet left it in the body of my woman, a Flathead who was gentle as the spring day and as warm as a hearth fire in winter. The Comanche warrior did this thing in the company of four Bannocks."

Buffalo Hump had heard all this before Hawk's arrival, Hawk realized, and did not comment. Hawk thought he saw reflected in the old chief's eyes a distaste for Two Hatchet's exploits with the Bannocks, though courtesy would not allow him to disparage the exploits of a warrior in his band.

"I have heard of the four Bannocks," Buffalo Hump admitted gravely. "I have heard too that they no longer collect scalps on this earth."

"That is true."

"Those who go against the golden-haired warrior do not fare well."

Hawk did not comment on this. It would not be seemly. The old chief had put it succinctly enough; there was no need for Hawk to embellish it. So he sat quietly, waiting for the arrival of Two Hatchet.

Buffalo Hump puffed for a while on his pipe, his obsidian eyes regarding Hawk intently. "Do not pay any attention to the woman of this old chief," he told Hawk abruptly. "It is not in her to forgive past wrongs. She is not as wise as a man. She is, after all, a woman." He puffed a while longer on his pipe, then removed the long stem from his wrinkled lips. "But this one holds her very dear. She warms his heart and keeps away the cold. Without her, he would be a tree without leaves, a desert without night."

The chief was telling Hawk that even if Hank-of-Hair did not wish to let bygones be bygones, he—Buffalo Hump—was perfectly willing to do so. What this meant was that if Hawk were willing, the enmity that had lasted for too long already between Hawk and the People of this band might finally end. Having come this far, hoping against hope to hear such words, Hawk felt his heart swell within him.

"The heart of this white man is glad to hear

what the wise chief of the Antelope Comanche says, that he is willing to forgive past wrongs. This white man is willing to do the same. There has been enough killing. This white man has been forced to kill many fine, brave Comanche warriors. It gave him only pain to do so."

"Yet the white man comes now to kill one more Comanche."

"No. This white man comes to give Two Hatchet what he journeyed so far to find, the scalp of this white man. He will stand before this Comanche warrior armed only with his knife. Two Hatchet may choose any weapon he wants. Two Hatchet will kill this white man or be killed by him and end this matter with honor." Hawk glanced slyly at the old chief. "Besides, such a combat will give the band a fine spectacle, an excuse for still another celebration—no matter who wins."

Buffalo Hump nodded gravely. "This old chief will see to it that the combat is fought fairly. When Two Hatchet comes to this lodge, this chief will tell him of the white warrior's decision. Surely Two Hatchet will be pleased to meet you in fair combat."

Hawk responded with a nod.

For a long while, Buffalo Hump puffed reflectively on his pipe. Then he took its stem from his mouth and spoke. "Does the white man know of his sister, Sky Woman?"

Hawk frowned. "Sky Woman is with the Shoshone. For two winters her brother has searched for her. He will find her yet."

The old chief took his pipe out of his mouth and spoke slowly, gravely, "When this great warrior, her brother, does find Sky Woman, perhaps he will tell her what is the truth for this old man—his heart is heavy still at her loss. A man does many foolish things in anger. Of all the fool deeds this aged one has done, sending away Sky Woman was the most foolish. Now, whenever these old eyes look upon the blue sky or gazes upon the sun-ripened grasses shifting in the wind, he thinks of Sky Woman and is filled with great sadness."

Impressed and deeply moved by Buffalo Hump's words, Hawk realized the old chief was asking both Hawk and Annabelle to accept his apology for having sold Annabelle—and for all that issued from that unfortunate act. Hawk let his head drop in polite acknowledgment of the old chief's sentiments; custom among the Plains tribes did not look favorably upon any who dwelled upon the heartfelt apology of another.

Hawk had achieved one goal at least: the long-standing enmity between this band and himself was gone forever. With Buffalo Hump's support and his own recent exploits in defense of the band, he was no longer the great scourge of the Antelope Comanches. Young Comanche braves might yet break away to seek their glory in taking Hawk's scalp, but that could not be helped. For this band at least, there would no longer be the same encouragement there had been in the past for such exploits.

Buffalo Hump took up his pipe and drew on it deeply, the smoke billowing about him, an indication that as far as he was concerned, the business between them had been settled. When Two Hatchet reported to the chief's lodge in answer to his summons, Buffalo Hump would see to the details concerning the combat.

Without further ceremony, Hawk got to his feet and left the tepee.

As he stepped clear of the lodge, Hank-of-Hair pulled up before him, her expression revealing pure malevolence. In a voice easily loud enough for her husband to hear from within his lodge, she announced that Two Hatchet was no longer in the village. He had fled, leaving his family and taking most of his earthly possessions with him on a single pack horse. She leaned back, her arms akimbo, her eyes gleaming in triumph.

The knowledge that Hawk would apparently not have his revenge on Two Hatchet filled her with pleasure. For his part, Hawk felt only a weary dismay.

— 10 —

Two Hatchet's trail petered out deep in the Rockies, close to the border of Bannock country. Hawk was not surprised. The renegade Comanche was seeking the aid and comfort of his old allies. Out of supplies, weary, Hawk returned to Fort Hall.

Alerted by the fort's guards, Mac Gregor met Hawk at the gate and drew him at once across the compound to his own Spartan apartment. There, he sat Hawk down before the fire and filled his glass with his best Scotch. Then he leaned back in his leather easy chair, waited for Hawk to drink his fill, and began his lament. "I tell ya, Hawk, it ain't the same. No, it ain't. Them beaver're gone from these valleys, an' even if they were still as thick as before, fashions have changed. That they have. Beaver hats are no longer what a bonnie gentleman wears today."

All this meant little to Hawk. He had never trapped or traded with anyone in this high country. All he had thought of was finding his sister and keeping his scalp on while he continued his search. But he gathered from the unhappy Scotsman's words that the Hudson's Bay Company was going to have a difficult time keeping its doors open if the mountain men and the surrounding Indians could not find enough beaver. Even if the company could get all the plews it needed, they still could not get a decent price for them.

Hawk nodded politely and sipped the molten fire called Scotch, and tried not to notice how much it made his head spin. He had not eaten much these past few days and the whiskey was slamming down into an empty stomach.

"I need supplies," Hawk told Mac Gregor. "I could kill some fresh meat for you in payment, if I could get some firing caps and powder."

"Suits me fine," said Mac Gregor eagerly. "We're running low on everything but salt pork, and I've long since had my fill of that. Been a long winter. That it has."

Hawk took another gulp of the whiskey. It was warming him clear to his bootheels. "The settlers are gone, I noticed."

"Yes, and good riddance. What a mess of pilgrims! Enough to try any man's patience, I'll tell you. Kids and dogs and families—all singin' of the Promised Land and not a one of them knowing what in hell's in store for them."

"Where's Jim?"

"He's leadin' the wagons, poor devil. Like he told you, it's Californy for him. He's been there before, and I reckon he knows what he's doin'. Only it seems to me Oregon's a long ways from Californy."

Hawk sipped his drink and thought over what Mac Gregor was telling him. Once more the wagon train would be attempting to make it through Grizzly Pass. The settlers would have to take that route if they were going to pick up their abandoned wagons—those that were still intact, that is.

Hawk did not ask about Alice Gentry. But he was thinking of her.

Less than a week later, Hawk found himself in charge of the fort's commissary. It was close to dusk and he was returning from his third hunt, leading his two, heavily laden pack horses. The elk and deer he had been slaughtering this past week had suffered through a miserable winter and did not dress down to much more than skin and bones. And this most recent kill was no different. But Mac Gregor was grateful for every ounce of fresh meat he could scrape from these bones, and so were the local blanket Indians who were now flocking back to the fort. Mac Gregor was lonely without the mountain men—now off with their traps—and the hordes of settlers he pretended to hate; he welcomed back these poor tobacco-store Indians with open arms.

As Hawk approached the fort, he thought the band of mounted Indians approaching him were coming from the fort to welcome him.

He was wrong.

As silently as thought they ringed him, forcing him to pull his own mount to a halt. One of the Indians nudged his horse closer. From his bearing and the color and manner of his dress, Hawk knew they were Shoshone, but from a mountain band he had never seen before this moment.

"You are Golden Hawk," the Indian said in excellent English.

Hawk nodded.

"I bring greetings from your sister, the golden-haired-one."

Hawk did not reply and did his best to remain calm. All these months he had searched for the band that held Annabelle, and now—without warning and without ceremony—here was that band seeking *him* out.

"You must come," the Shoshone said.

"What are you called?" Hawk demanded. His question was ill-mannered, but this moment was too important for him to wait on ceremony.

The Shoshone did not appear to be offended. "I am Crow Wing. Golden Hawk's sister is my woman. I have come to take you to her."

There was something in Crow Wing's voice that alerted Hawk to trouble. Cold fear caught at his throat. "What is wrong with my sister?"

"Since the late winter winds, the cold devils have taken her. They sit on her chest and do not let her breathe, and they build a fire within her. But she will not let our healers cure her. Over and over she calls out for you. Sometimes she sees you at the foot of her couch and tries to go with you. It takes many women and braves to hold her down. You must come. If you do not, we will not be able to help her."

"How far is your village?"

"Two nights, three days."

"I will come," Hawk told him at once. Then he looked back at the two laden pack horses. "This meat must be delivered to the fort."

Crow's Wing turned and spoke in Shoshone to a brave beside him. The brave nudged his pony alongside Hawk's, took from Hawk's hand the lead holding the two pack horses, then turned his pony about and headed toward the fort.

Hawk had no doubt the Shoshone would deliver the meat to Mac Gregor, who would have to wait a long, long while for an explanation.

Hawk stooped and entered the tepee. The women tending his sister quickly stepped to one side. He looked down at Annabelle and for a terrible moment thought he had come too late. Her pale features had been rendered skeletal by the virulent pneumonia that held her in its thrall. A racking cough broke occasionally from her pale, bloodless lips. Her eyes, closed now in fitful sleep, were sunken; her long golden hair, pale and without luster, clung damply to her feverish forehead. She looked so frail it seemed that a harsh word would be enough to crush her into dust.

Beside her couch sat a tin cup, a gourd filled with water next to it. Hawk knelt by his sister, filled the cup with water, and held it close to her lips, so close its cold rim rested against one of them.

"Annabelle," he called softly, urgently.

There was no response.

"It's me! Jed," he told her.

He thought she stirred, but could not be sure. Glancing up, he saw the tribe's medicine man enter, his bag of herbs in one hand, a rattle in the other. Hawk caught the Indian's eyes with his own, and with their force alone stopped the medicine man in his tracks. Slowly, silently, the medicine man withdrew.

Hawk looked back at Annabelle, leaned close, and kissed her on the forehead. Then, very softly, he called her name. This time she stirred and turned her head slightly in his direction. Again Hawk held the cold tin cup to her lips. She opened them. He let a small portion of the ice-cold water trickle over her lower lip and into her mouth. She swallowed and opened her eyes.

"I'm here, Annabelle," Hawk said.

She turned her head all the way and saw him. Wonder, then joy filled her eyes. With a tiny, feeble cry she lifted her arms toward him. He hugged her eagerly, appalled by the feverish heat emanating from her frail body. She was virtually on fire. And her bones seemed as easy to crush as those of a sparrow.

Hawk pulled away to see what could be done for her.

"Stay," Annabelle cried, close to panic.

He smiled at her and said, "I am not going anywhere, Annabelle. I'll be right here. As long as you need me. That's a promise."

Closing her eyes, Annabelle sank back onto her couch and appeared to sleep.

In Kentucky as a young boy of eleven, Hawk had come down with pneumonia himself. He remembered the terrible, tearing cough, the sense that a stone lay on his chest, the incontinence that so embarrassed him, and how close he came to death as he slipped, for longer and longer periods, from consciousness into darkness. And he remembered too the little old lady from a hollow many miles away who had come in with her bag late one night to tend to him and her sharp, birdlike eyes as she regarded him. She had said not a word to him. But once her strong, bony hands rested for a moment on his forehead, he knew he would be well.

Now Hawk applied to his sister those same tactics that had saved him.

Using Crow Wing as his interpreter, Hawk directed the women tending Annabelle to wrap her in heavy blankets and then to increase the fire in the tepee. It was obvious they did not approve, but they obeyed quickly. Then Hawk told the women to see to it that he had plenty of water on hand for his sister, after which, as the temperature in the tepee climbed to an almost unbearable level, he took her hand and hung on—as the old woman had taken his hand so many years before.

Her frail person almost hidden completely by the pile of furs and blankets thrown over her, Annabelle began to stir fitfully. The heat in her hand was almost enough to sear his palm. She was on fire, it seemed. It was a wonder to Hawk that she had not yet ignited her couch. Her delirium increased. She cried out. Sometimes she screamed. But each time, she responded to Hawk's calming voice, drank the water he pressed to her lips, then sank once more into a fitful sleep.

Hawk lost track of time. He remembered dimly the procession of exhausted women entering and leaving. He felt at times as if he too were delirious as the grim, impassive faces of the old women and men peered at him and his sister. Twice more the medicine man appeared in the entrance, but each time Crow Wing was on hand to restrain him gently and send him on his way.

Close to dawn Hawk became aware that the heat in Annabelle's hand was no longer quite as intense. He peered more closely at his sister and for the first time saw tiny beads of perspiration covering her forehead and face. Leaning over, he placed his hand on her forehead. It came away wet with perspiration.

The fever had broken!

Speaking quickly to Crow Wing, he instructed the women to take the blankets and furs off Annabelle. They did so and found she was soaking wet. She stirred as they exchanged dry bedding for the wet and then opened her eyes to gaze on Hawk.

"It was not a dream," she said to him softly. "You *are* here!"

"Yes," he said. "Crow Wing brought me."

"I feel very weak, but I am better, am I not?"

"Yes, much better. The fever has passed."

"Now I will live," she told Hawk wonderingly. "For a long while I paused between this world and that. But I am content to return."

"Sleep, then. Get your strength back."

She nodded and looked toward Crow Wing. He started eagerly for her, then waited for Hawk to move back. Kneeling by her side, he kissed her with great tenderness on her forehead. Her smile in response was beautiful. There was no doubt in Hawk's mind that Annabelle loved this Shoshone warrior very much and that he loved her just as deeply in return.

It should not have surprised him, and it didn't. What he felt instead was shock.

A week later Annabelle was well enough to leave her tepee and visit with Hawk. They found a log overlooking a ravine. Spring was almost upon them, and the sound of the swift, snow-fed waters rushing through the narrow gorge so far below them was soothing. A fresh, gentle breeze blew through Annabelle's hair as her swift fingers braided the long, golden strands into two bulky braids.

Her attempt to explain matters was not going

well. When Hawk asked her to come away with him—to go back to St. Louis and from there to the land of their Kentucky ancestors—she told him that would be impossible. When he pressed her, demanding to know why, she told him.

She was carrying Crow Wing's child.

"It will be a boy," she said, her eyes bright with expectation. "He moves about so. All the women say this."

"Then it will be a boy. And we will bring it up, but not as a Shoshone, as a white boy in a white civilization."

"Do you really mean that, Jed?"

He thought a moment, then shook his head. "No," he said, "I guess not. Even as I spoke, I thought better of it. I am confused. I have looked so long and so hard to find you—and now that I have, you do not wish to return with me. After all, it was you who made me promise."

"If I were not bearing Crow Wing's child, I would go back."

"No, you wouldn't."

"What do you mean?"

"You love Crow Wing, and he loves you."

She looked quickly away from Hawk, her face flushing, not with anger but with embarrassment. "Are you ashamed of me for that?" she asked, her voice small.

"I do not know."

"He is a savage, and now I am one too because I find pleasure in his arms—like any other Shoshone woman. Is that what you think?"

Before he could reply, she got up from the log and walked hurriedly back to her tepee. Hawk watched her go, feeling helpless and inept. He knew what he should have said. Only now it was too late.

Crow Wing had been watching them, but had kept a respectful distance. Now he hurried over. "I would speak with Golden Hawk."

"Speak."

"Your sister is my woman. You have brought her back to me. One day she will bear our son. We of the Shoshone consider you our brother now."

"Thank you, Crow Wing."

"It is said you still seek the Comanche who killed your woman."

"I do."

"And he is called Two Hatchet."

"You know where he is?"

"He is with the Bannock. Two Hatchet is one who must use others. He has found in the Bannock a people who appreciate his talent for trickery and deceit."

"I already guessed he was with them, Crow Wing."

"And did you guess they would attack the wagon train that left the fort this month."

"No," Hawk replied, astonished. "I did not."

"Once again the settlers are trapped not far from here in the pass your people call Grizzly Pass. But this time it is not snow that stops them, but the Bannocks, led by Two Hatchet."

At once Hawk thought of Jim Clyman trying to fight off the Bannock warriors while the settlers, like chickens with their roost invaded by foxes, did nothing more than squawk, flutter about, and get in the way.

And then he thought of Alice Gentry.

Hawk stood on a ledge overlooking the floor of the pass. Behind him crouched Crow Wing and about thirty Shoshone warriors. There had been some pretty intense gunfire about an hour before they reached this ledge, but since then the firing had calmed down considerably. It looked as if the attacking warriors were content to take cover on the slopes and pick away at the wagons and the settlers huddling in them.

Many of the wagons had been rebuilt, four of them completely, from the look of them. The men were scurrying about behind the wagons, with most of the women and children huddled under them. One wagon farther down the pass had been hit by fire arrows and was now a smoldering ruin. A few settlers were sprawled facedown on this side of the pass, arrows sticking in them like pins in a pincushion. Evidently the Bannock fire had been too murderous to allow the settlers to retrieve their bodies or do anything to aid them in the event that any of them were still alive.

With a wave of his hand, Hawk sent the Shoshone out in a wide arc. Like a net falling upon an unsuspecting school of fish, the Shoshone fell upon the Bannock warriors. So intent were the Bannocks on what scalps and goods lay before them, they had allowed themselves to be taken in the rear.

In his hand Hawk held the lance Two Hatchet had left behind in Singing Wind's body. He had broken it into three pieces and now carried in his belt the end with the steel tip. As he glided down the steep slope, his eyes searching for some sign of Two Hatchet, a Bannock stepped out in front of him.

If the Bannock had been surprised to see Hawk, he did not show it as he flung his hatchet at Hawk. Hawk ducked, reached back, and let fly his throwing knife. The blade caught the Bannock in the chest. He sagged forward onto his knees, and before he pitched forward onto the knife hilt, he let out a fierce warning cry to his fellow Bannock warriors.

Hawk leapt forward, pressed the dying man down onto his knife, then flung him aside, retrieved the knife, and charged on down the steep slope. It was now alive with Bannocks. But so too was it alive with Shoshone warriors. The hand-to-hand fighting was intense, and Hawk's knife drank deep of Bannock blood as he fought his way down the slope—a wild, blond-haired demon of destruction, moving from one Bannock warrior to another with the speed of a great and deadly bird of prey.

Meanwhile, Jim Clyman and the others, realizing almost immediately what was happening, left the wagons and swarmed across the floor of the pass and up both slopes to join in the fighting. In less than an hour, the Bannock warriors—caught between the aroused settlers coming at them from below and the Shoshone Indians swarming down upon them from above—fled the pass in such a panic they did not even pause long enough to take their dead with them.

Hawk helped a wounded Shoshone brave to his feet. The warrior had an arrow wound in his forearm. It was not fatal and its scar would make him a hero to all the young women of the tribe. This was the only explanation for the proud grin on his face. Hawk, near the floor of the pass by this time, glanced across it to watch Jim Clyman and the men being welcomed back by their women and children. Hawk tried to pick out Alice Gentry, but could not.

Then, from around a boulder, stepped a Comanche warrior.

Two Hatchet.

— 11 —

Behind Two Hatchet appeared three Shoshone warriors. One of them was Crow Wing. It was he who nudged the wary Comanche closer to Hawk.

"I told this one he would live only if he stayed to fight Golden Hawk," said Crow Wing.

With a grim nod, Hawk strode toward Two Hatchet.

"Let me warn you," said Crow Wing. "When a Shoshone brave helped him to his feet earlier, this Comanche killed the brave with a single knife thrust to the stomach. Be careful, Golden Hawk."

"Just stand aside." Hawk took from his waistband the head of the lance he had been carrying for so long. The moment he saw the gleaming lance blade in Hawk's hand, Two Hatchet crouched, determined to sell his life dearly. In one hand he held a long skinning knife. Stuck in his breech-clout's belt was a flintlock pistol.

Hawk drew back the lance. Two Hatchet did not wait. He rushed Hawk, who flung the lance and caught Two Hatchet in the shoulder. Though it dug in cruelly and then glanced off, the force of its impact was enough to stagger Two Hatchet. Hawk unsheathed his bowie and darted in to finish off the Comanche—and found himself staring into the muzzle of a Walker Colt, the same weapon he had left with Singing Wind.

The gun detonated, its round slamming into Hawk's left shoulder, spinning him brutally about. He struck the ground. Again the Colt thundered; this time the round nicked Hawk's ear. Rolling over quickly, Hawk found himself staring up at Two Hatchet as he thumb-cocked the Walker for the third time.

Hawk came up onto one knee, then lunged with his bowie. The blade sank into Two Hatchet's gut. Dropping the Colt, the Comanche grabbed at his vitals, blood pouring from between his grasping fingers. In a moment, gasping, he had sunk into a black pool of his own blood.

Hawk pushed himself erect. He had the odd feeling that his left side was no longer a part of him, that he had left it somewhere. He picked up the head of the lance, then walked shakily over to Two Hatchet, kicked him onto his back, then buried the long iron tip into the Comanche's heart.

It should have made Hawk feel better. He had

finally avenged Singing Wind's death, and he had done it with the same lance Two Hatchet had used to kill her. It should have been enough to satisfy him.

But it wasn't. Singing Wind was still dead.

He became very dizzy. The world spun about him alarmingly. He sank to the ground and looked up to see an anxious Jim Clyman rushing toward him, Alice Gentry on his heels.

The constant creak and roll of the wagons lulled Hawk for days as he fought to regain his strength. He was in Alice Gentry's wagon, and for the most part, it was she who looked after him. By the time they had crossed the divide and put Grizzly Pass well behind them, Hawk was sitting up on the seat, taking turns driving the horses.

Jim rode by constantly to check on Hawk's condition. When it appeared that Hawk now had a sound-enough mind to make decisions for himself, both Jim and Alice began doing all they could to entice him to make his home in Oregon or California, to settle down and farm, as his folks had done back in Kentucky and as they had planned to do in Texas before the Comanches wiped them out.

They both presented a powerful argument to Hawk, Alice Gentry speaking as much with her body as with words. Hawk did not know if it was the lure of a new unspoiled land yet to be settled that was convincing him, or the lure of Alice Gentry's warm, sensual body. It wasn't long before he decided it didn't make all that much difference.

And so he decided to tell Alice of his decision.

They had halted for the night. The evening meal was done, the swarms of children collected and put to bed. A few of the settlers were strolling among the wagons, talking softly, excitedly, about the new land ahead of them.

Hawk paused beside a boulder and gazed down a steep slope at a stream far below, the rising moon sending flakes of silver across it at one point. Alice seemed unusually beautiful. She was wearing a long blue gown she had put on after bathing in the stream directly after supper. Her hair and body smelled as sweet as apple blossoms, and Hawk realized it was time for him to tell her what he had decided.

He cleared his throat to get her attention.

She smiled at him. "I know. You've been aching to tell me something all evening. Go on. What is it?"

"I've decided to go to Oregon with you."

With a delighted cry, she flung herself into his arms. "Does that mean you and I . . . I mean, that we'll be getting married."

He grinned at her. "As soon as we can find a preacher."

"Oh, Jed! You won't be sorry. I promise you."

"And neither will you, Alice. I'll work hard. I'll put the wilderness behind me. Like my father and his people, I'll return to the soil. I'll rip open the earth and reap what I sow."

"And we'll have children."

"Of course."

"And that means you're renouncing your savage past. All of it! Isn't that so, Jed?"

He looked at her closely, frowning. He was not sure what she was getting at. "What do you mean, Alice?"

"I mean, you're renouncing that untutored savage you lived with, the one Jim Clyman told me about."

"You mean Singing Wind?"

"Yes, that Flathead squaw you bedded while you lived in Jim's cabin. Jim said there was no marriage. He said you just took her in."

"That's right. There was no marriage."

"Well, I want you to know I don't care, Jed. That ugly business is all behind you now. I forgive you. Others warned me that you were living with a savage heathen, but I told them I was willing to let that pass and say no more about it. That's fair enough, isn't it, Jed?"

Hawk looked long and hard at her. "Yes," he said at length. "That is fair, Alice. And I am grateful you're willing to forgive me."

She hugged him again, then kissed him on the lips, hard. "Oh, my! You've made me so happy, Jed."

"Because I am putting my savage past behind me and am joining you in making a new, civilized life in Oregon. Is that it?"

"Yes, Jed. That's it."

"I see."

She frowned. "Jed, is there anything wrong?"

He looked at her with sudden concern. "It's getting chilly," he told her. "I think I'd better escort you back to the wagon."

She hugged his arm. "Yes," she told him eagerly, "and before long we'll make each other a whole lot warmer than we are now."

Hawk said nothing, and when they reached Alice's wagon, he helped her up into it.

"Give me a little time to make the bed," she told him.

"How much time?"

"Fifteen minutes."

He nodded.

With a wave, Alice vanished into the wagon.

About fifteen minutes later, Hawk, astride his horse, stopped beside Jim Clyman's fire at the head of the wagon train. Jim was greasing his wagon's rear axle. He stood up, brushed his hands off on the thick, damp grass, and stared up at Hawk questioningly.

"Going somewhere?" he asked.

"Back to Grizzly Pass—and Annabelle."

"Right now?"

"Right now—as long as the moon holds, anyway."

"Kind of sudden, ain't it?"

"It is that. Jim, I want to thank you for all

you've done—and thank Alice for me, too, will you?"

"Shouldn't you do that yourself?"

"I'd rather you did it for me. And take care of her. Maybe you could talk her into going with you to California."

Jim's eyes gleamed. "Now, that's not a bad idea."

"And tell her for me, Jim, that I'm glad she could forgive me, but I just couldn't forgive myself."

"That don't make much sense, Hawk."

"It will to Alice."

Hawk turned his horse and rode out. The moon was bright enough for him to see the freshly rutted trail they had cut through the spring wilderness that day, and before long he could feel his mount lifting into the high country once more, heading back for the Continental Divide.

He found himself whistling softly. He was like a man released from a debilitating spell. Thinking back on Alice, he was reminded of the Greek enchantress Old Bill Williams had told him about once. Her name was Circe, and she turned men into swine.

Alice had almost succeeded in doing that to him.

But he was willing to forgive her, just as she was willing to forgive him. And now, at the moment, all Hawk wanted was to see his sister again. He had something he wanted to tell her, something he would have told her earlier if she had not run off like that. What he had wanted to say was that the Shoshone were her people now, as much as any kin of hers in Kentucky.

As for Hawk, he was not sure who his people were, not now. Were they the whites he despised, or the savages with whom he fought and would keep on fighting for as long as the scalp belonging to the one they called Golden Hawk was a trophy worth taking.

Read all the titles in
THE INDIAN HERITAGE SERIES
by Paul Lederer

☐ **BOOK ONE: MANITOU'S DAUGHTERS**—Manitou was the god of the proud Oneidas, and these were the tribes' chosen daughters: Crenna, the strongest and wisest, who lost her position when she gave herself to the white man; Kala, beautiful and wanton, found her perfect match in the Englishman as ruthless as she; and Sachim, young and innocent, was ill-prepared for the tide of violence and terror that threatened to ravish their lands ... Proud women of a proud people—facing the white invaders of their land and their hearts.... (138317—$3.50)

☐ **BOOK TWO: SHAWNEE DAWN**—William and Cara Van der Veghe were raised by their white father and Indian mother deep in the wilderness. But when the tide of white settlement crept closer, William and Cara had to choose sides on the frontier, he with the whites, she with the Shawnee. Brother and sister, bound together by blood, now facing each other over the flames of violence and vengeance.... (138325—$3.50)

☐ **BOOK THREE: SEMINOLE SKIES**—Shanna and her younger sister Lychma were fleeing the invading white men when they fell into even more feared hands—those of the ruthless Seminoles. But Shanna would not be broken, for she had the blood of a princess in her veins. Then she met the legendary warrior, Yui, the one man strong enough to save his people from white conquest—and to turn a woman's burning hate into flaming love.... (122631—$2.95)

☐ **BOOK FOUR: CHEYENNE DREAM**—Amaya's dream to help the proud Cheyenne people live in peace was dissolving into a sea of blood as white settlers broke their paper treaties. now, she fears the one white man who can save her people may be asking a price she is not prepared to pay.... (136519—$3.50)

☐ **BOOK FIVE: THE WAY OF THE WIND**—Born a Cheyenne, and given by her mother to the whites, she became Mary Hart. But in the arms of a great warrior chief, she became Akton, the name of her birth, educating her people, and loving without limit as she was born to do.... (140389—$3.50)

Prices slightly higher in Canada.